PRAISE FOR ELLEN SUSSMAN

Praise for *A Wedding in Provence*

"A lighthearted tale of love, trust, secrets and family. [The story is] told with intimate authority and against the backdrop of southern France. . . . Sussman brings the countryside to life with her rich narrative."

—*Bookreporter*

"Women's fiction fans will enjoy Sussman's . . . knowing exploration of mother/daughter relationships and the bond between sisters. The vivid descriptions of Provence will whisk the reader away to the Mediterranean tout suite."

—*Library Journal*

"A couple plans for a low-key wedding in the French country-side and gets anything but: The bride's children from her previous marriage are ready to let loose, and so is the best man. Sussman fills her comédie with plenty of insight about love, loss and intimacy."

—*Good Housekeeping*

"*A Wedding in Provence* is a rich novel. . . . The depth of relationships and histories of the characters, individually and together, make this novel both reflective and hopeful. A great read about what it means to truly stick together through thick and thin."

—*Romantic Times Book Review*

Praise for *The Paradise Guest House*

"[A] story of healing and redemption, of finding love in the most unexpected places, and of the importance of moving forward . . . Sussman has drawn a vivid, well-balanced portrait of a woman and a country working to recover from an unimaginable event and a very personal look at a global tragedy."

—*Booklist*

"[A] moving story about making sense of life after a tragedy . . . This touching tale will cause contemplation about what closure truly means."

—*Romantic Times Book Reviews*

"With well-drawn, genuinely likable lead characters, [*The Paradise Guest House*] takes readers on an edgy island adventure over memorable emotional terrain."

—Associated Press

"Echoing Bali's difficult recovery from [the 2002 terrorist bombing], the characters tread the difficult terrain of post-traumatic attachment. . . . A respectful and earnest . . . treatment of devastation's aftermath."

—*Kirkus Reviews*

Praise for *French Lessons*

"[A] luscious novel of love and longing . . . the narrative feels as light as a glass of rosé at an outdoor café, but its insights carry the richness of a Burgundy."

—*People* (four stars)

"[A] sexy travelogue . . . sizzling escapist reading."

—*Entertainment Weekly*

"[An] evocative escape to the City of Love."

—*Kirkus Reviews*

"Charming, romantic, and brimming with Sussman's trademark joie de vivre, *French Lessons* is a novel to savor."

—AMANDA EYRE WARD, author of *How to Be Lost*

BY ELLEN SUSSMAN

A Wedding in Provence

The Paradise Guest House

French Lessons

On a Night Like This

Bad Girls: 26 Writers Misbehave

Dirty Words: A Literary Encyclopedia of Sex

A Wedding in Provence

BALLANTINE BOOKS

NEW YORK

A Wedding in Provence

A Novel

ELLEN SUSSMAN

2015 Ballantine Books Trade Paperback Edition

Copyright © 2014 by Ellen Sussman
Reading group guide copyright © 2015 by
Penguin Random House LLC

Published in the United States by Ballantine Books,
an imprint of Random House, a division of
Penguin Random House LLC, New York.

BALLANTINE and the HOUSE colophon are registered
trademarks of Penguin Random House LLC.

RANDOM HOUSE READER'S CIRCLE & Design is a registered
trademark of Penguin Random House LLC.

Originally published in hardcover in the United States
by Ballantine Books, an imprint of Random House,
a division of Penguin Random House LLC, in 2015.

LIBRARY OF CONGRESS CATALOGING-IN-PUBLICATION DATA
Sussman, Ellen
A wedding in Provence : a novel / Ellen Sussman.
pages cm
ISBN 978-0-345-54897-9
eBook ISBN 978-0-345-54896-2
1. Man-woman relationships—Fiction. 2. Weddings—Fiction.
I. Title.
PS3619.U845W44 2014
813'.6—dc23
2014017533

Printed in the United States of America on acid-free paper

www.randomhousereaderscircle.com

9 8 7 6 5 4 3 2

Book design by Dana Leigh Blanchette
Title-page, epigraph, and part-title images: © iStockphoto.com

For Neal, my love

Come to France.

STAY AT OUR FRIENDS' LOVELY INN IN CASSIS,

A TOWN ON THE MEDITERRANEAN.

JOIN US AS WE JOIN TOGETHER IN MARRIAGE.

OUR WEDDING WILL TAKE PLACE ON

SUNDAY, JUNE 22, 2014 AT 5 P.M.

IN THE GARDEN OF LA MAISON VERTE.

PLEASE STAY FOR THE WEEKEND.

WE'D LIKE TO BRING OUR CLOSEST FRIENDS

AND FAMILY TOGETHER FOR THIS OCCASION.

WE'LL CELEBRATE LIKE CRAZY.

Part One

Chapter One

"I need to see the Mediterranean," Olivia said.

The road from Marseille had taken them through a long claustrophobic tunnel and then into the sprawl of developments on the edge of the city. Boxy cement structures that housed apartments sprouted at the top of every hill. The roads were crowded, the drivers aggressive.

Something kept clicking in the rental car, a persistent, irritating sound that put Olivia on edge. She and Brody had tried to identify the source—a seat belt, the radio, an unlatched glove compartment—but nothing seemed connected to the noise. They drowned it out with bad French rock and roll.

"Should we take a beach detour?" Brody asked, pushing up his sleeves.

"Please," Olivia said.

Brody followed the exit ramp until it deposited them on a busy street. Then he glanced at Olivia. "Is this better?"

No. McDonald's on their right, a fast-food pizza joint on their left. The air thick with the smell of grease. A long stretch of apartment buildings, many spray-painted with red devils holding guns.

"There's a sign for Cassis," Brody said, pointing.

"Take it!" Olivia said.

They followed a new road that climbed the hills, leaving the overdeveloped city behind. Soon mountains stretched ahead of them, white rock, red rock, pine forest.

"For weeks now I've been dreaming about the big blue sea and the waves washing against the sand," Olivia said.

"There aren't usually any waves here. It's as calm as can be."

"Don't ruin my fantasy," Olivia said, cuffing his shoulder.

"Look," Brody said.

They crested the hill and the sea appeared before them. The sun glinted off Brody's watch, momentarily blinding Olivia. She blinked. The car turned slightly, and finally she could see the bay, bordered by sheer limestone cliffs.

"My big blue sea!" she called.

"No waves," Brody said.

"I don't need them."

"My wedding gift to you," Brody said, opening an arm to the vista.

"You're so generous," she told him.

She loved his wide mouth, his deep-set eyes. She never got tired of looking at him. He was handsome in a rugged way; she could see Wyoming in his tall, lanky body, his strong hands, the crow's-feet in the corner of his eyes.

The road descended quickly, leading them onto a small road that wound its way to the coast. Brody found a parking space near the beach path, and Olivia bounded out of the car, eager to feel the sea breeze against her damp skin. They climbed down a well-worn trail and stepped out onto a rocky beach.

Only a few people sat in the late-day sun, which perched on top of a jagged cliff, still dazzling. A couple of children played in the surf and one man swam out to sea, his body slicing through the water.

"It's beautiful," Brody said.

"It's perfect," Olivia said, taking his hand.

She heard a bark, followed by a fury of yelps and howls. She spun around. From a cove a few hundred feet to their left, two large dogs charged toward them. The first, a German shepherd, locked fierce eyes on her. Are they just chasing each other? she thought. No, they're heading right at me.

Scream. Open your mouth and scream.

But her body tightened and no words escaped her lips. They'll kill me, she thought.

And then in a rush of mad thoughts, she began to make wishes. What I want before I die: I want to marry Brody. I want a life with him, a long life. And my daughters! I want Carly to ditch her boyfriend. I want Nell to stop fighting against the world. I want to see what happens next in their lives, the men they marry, the women they become. As if time had stopped, the dogs still raced toward her, their enormous jaws wet with anticipation. The sound of her own heart pounded in her ears.

And then Brody stepped forward and she heard murmuring sounds, gentle coos, words that weren't words at all. He kept walking toward the beasts, speaking some other language, animal language. The shepherd cocked his head, looking at Brody now, as if he just discovered the most interesting creature in the world. Just like that, Olivia was forgotten.

The German shepherd stopped. Brody put out his hand and the dog sniffed it warily. He kept talking and now Olivia could hear words: "Good dog, hey buddy, what's going on, pal."

The other dog, a lean black Lab, circled them but didn't come closer.

"I thought I was dinner," Olivia said in a small voice.

"He would have picked me first," Brody said, petting the dog, which seemed to shrink in size. "I'd be much tastier."

"I couldn't scream," she told him.

"Good," he said. "Screaming would have been a bad idea."

"You weren't scared?"

He shook his head. "They weren't going to hurt anyone." He patted the dog's haunches. "Were you, good boy?"

Of course, Olivia thought. It's what he does. Or what he did. He had been a large-animal vet when they met over a year before. But he'd quit his job three months earlier, along with Wyoming, when he moved to be with her in San Francisco. She'd barely known him in his landscape of mountains and beasts.

"You need to do this," she said quietly.

"Save you from puppies?"

She put her hand on his shoulder. "Work with animals."

"I've been looking. If I can't find work as a vet I'll find something else to do," he said assuredly. But he hadn't had any luck in three months of trying. She worried that he needed Wyoming in some essential way.

The German shepherd rambled over to Olivia and she stiffened.

"Easy, boy," Brody said. "Be gentle with my bride."

The dog sniffed and then pushed his nose against Olivia's side. She petted him warily. He moved his nose to her hip and nipped her.

"He bit me!" Olivia said, though she wasn't quite sure what it was. A love bite? A warning?

"Hugo! Lulu!" a voice yelled, and the two dogs ran off, bounding along the beach, heading toward the open arms of a teenager emerging from the sea.

Olivia rubbed her hip. There was no pain, just a wet spot where the dog's mouth had been.

"Are you okay?" Brody asked.

Olivia nodded. "I'm fine. I'm wonderful."

They watched as the black Lab knocked the boy back into the water and all three of them splashed through the waves until they were swimming, two dog heads and one boy head bobbing on the turquoise sea.

"You know what makes me unbearably sad?" she said, wrapping her arms around her body, suddenly chilled. "I wish we were twenty. I wish we'd never loved anyone before. I wish you didn't have a dead wife and I didn't have an awful ex. I wish we had fifty years ahead of us instead—"

Her voice broke. Brody stepped up behind her and took her

in his arms. He pressed her back against his chest, leaned his chin on her head.

"It took all those years to bring us to this weekend," he said. "We needed the wrong turns and the detours and the false starts. Look where we ended up."

"My big blue sea," Olivia said.

"Marry me," Brody said.

Olivia walked into the garden of La Maison Verte, expecting to find Emily already there. She had told Brody that she'd head downstairs early so she could steal a few minutes with her best friend. She sat in one of the wrought-iron chairs and within a few minutes, Ulysse, Emily and Sébastien's white retriever, padded over and dropped to the ground at her feet. This one's not ferocious, she thought. She petted him and whispered *"Bonsoir, Monsieur Ulysse,"* into his ear. He put his head down but his wagging tail swept the tiny stones on the path behind him.

Olivia leaned back in her chair and looked around. The inn and gardens were exquisite, no doubt due to her friend's remarkable sense of style. Emily had never run a country inn before, much less one in the south of France, but she had always been able to transform any space into a place that invited you to linger. Look around. Breathe. She even had that skill at twenty when they'd been roommates at Berkeley. Their small suite was every friend's favorite hiding place thanks to Emily's found art, wallpaper made from magazine collages, furniture covered with tapestries.

Now she had become mistress of the manor, though this

place looked more like a hidden jewel. The house was covered with ivy, and the stucco walls were painted a rusted orange color as surprising as it was pleasing. The building twisted and turned so that here in the garden Olivia felt as if the house had taken her in its arms. And the garden itself was both lush and bursting with color, though somehow it calmed rather than assaulted the soul.

She considered the champagne bottle resting on ice in the glass bowl but decided against it. Linger. Look around. Breathe.

Soon she'd give up breathing. Her daughters were due to arrive tomorrow morning along with Brody's mother and Jake, his best friend. Jake, the cowboy who hated marriage, would perform the wedding ceremony. Why had Brody insisted on that? Would the guy take it seriously? Give it up, Olivia told herself. You already agreed.

Now she felt an undercurrent of fear, like an itchy scalp, that this wedding in France was fraught with peril. For starters there were her daughters: One was a mess; the other wouldn't mess up. Brody's parents: His father had walked out on their fifty-five-year marriage a couple of months before and no one could understand why. Fanny was coming to the wedding but not Sam, who had cut off all contact with everyone. And then Brody's best friend, Jake: Well, he had warned Brody against marrying Olivia.

Linger. Look around. Breathe.

The inn was tucked into a valley; vineyards carpeted the land as far as Olivia could see. Late evening light bathed the hills so that the many shades of green seemed to vibrate and shimmer. Towering above them stood Cap Canaille, a cliff of red rock that ran along the edge of the valley and jutted out into the Mediterranean.

Tonight they were alone at the inn with Emily and Sébastien, her French husband, whom Olivia adored. Tonight she'd sleep with Brody in that gorgeous room in the inn and they'd forget about everyone else. Tonight she'd drink champagne.

"The bride," Emily said and Olivia startled, sending Ulysse into a flurry of movement and barking and flying stones.

"He's me," Olivia said. "That's what I'd be doing if I weren't so well behaved."

"Since when are you well behaved?"

"Can we open that champagne without waiting for the guys?"

"Same old O," Emily said. Only Emily called Olivia O. Once Brody had tried it and Olivia silenced him: "Find your own nickname," she had told him. Olivia is Olivia to everyone in the world except Emily. And Emily, of course, is Em.

"I'm rattled," Olivia said. "I know you think this is a good idea. Want to let me in on the reason?"

"For a wedding?" Emily opened the champagne while Olivia held out two glasses.

"For a wedding with guests."

"You want me to leave?"

"I want everyone else to leave. And they haven't even gotten here yet."

Emily poured the champagne. "It will be wonderful," she said. "You don't have to do anything but drink champagne for three straight days."

"Deal."

Both women dropped into their chairs, side by side. Olivia leaned over and clinked glasses again with Emily.

"To you. To your beautiful inn. To your amazing generosity."

"To our friendship."

"You guys getting married?" someone called and both women spun around.

Brody walked down the path toward them, the sun low in the sky behind him. He wore a pale blue shirt, jeans, his cowboy boots. Olivia felt her heart ease.

"I'm pathetically straight," she said. "Otherwise I would have run off with this woman years ago."

"Thank God," Brody said. "Have you finished the champagne?"

Emily stood and reached for the bottle.

"First, good evening," Brody said. He leaned forward and kissed Emily on both cheeks. Then he walked to Olivia, pulled her up and into his arms.

"Good evening, my love," Olivia said. "You look very handsome."

"You're just trying to seduce me into marrying you," Brody said.

Emily handed him a glass and they all clinked and drank.

"I love you guys," Emily said. "Who finds love at our age?"

Olivia was fifty-five, Brody was fifty-two. She had met him when her theater company was on tour across the country. As artistic director, she tagged along for the first few shows because a battle was brewing between the director and the actors. After a performance in Laramie one night, Olivia had gone for a drink at the Old Buckhorn Bar and ended up sitting next to a man who was reading a novel while everyone else was downing shots of whiskey. Now, they were getting married.

"Emily!" Sébastien called from the inn. Ulysse bounded toward him.

"Our master calls," Emily said and headed back down the path.

Brody leaned over and kissed Olivia's head. "Marry me," he said. He'd been saying it for months, ever since he asked her and she said yes. He claimed to like the sound of it on his lips, her expression each time he asked her, and the certainty he had that she'd say yes. Yes.

"*Et voilà!*" Emily called.

She walked up the path, a tray of aperitifs in her hands, followed by Sébastien who carried two bottles of wine. Ulysse shadowed him, almost bouncing as he walked. Happy old dog as long as his people were near.

Olivia greeted Sébastien with a kiss on each cheek; Brody threw one arm around his back. Brody had met Emily and Sébastien a couple of months earlier when they'd closed down the inn and traveled to San Francisco for a week's vacation. Olivia had loved the ease with which her old best friends and the new guy in her life forged instant friendships.

"I've come to tell you all about *le mariage*," Sébastien said.

The others groaned.

"We have years of experience! We have wisdom! We have wine!"

"Spare me," Olivia said.

She had been married for twenty-two years to a man who had lost himself in his work. After she finally left him seven years ago, she thought she'd never marry again. She already had kids; she was too old for more. Even after she met Brody she didn't consider marriage. She lived in California—lots of people had a significant other or a partner in their lives. When Brody had proposed, on the top of a mountain near Tahoe, she was shocked and wildly pleased. Marriage? At our age? Yes!

"Who else will give you advice?" Sébastien persisted. "We'll start with the wedding night."

"No!" Olivia shouted. "Not that! My virgin ears!"

Sébastien poured himself the last of the champagne and toasted them. "To hot married sex!" he proclaimed.

They all settled into their chairs and Emily passed around the small bowls of olives, tapenade on toast, crisp potato chips.

"This is your life?" Brody asked. "Every day?"

"Not even close," Emily said. "We wake up to breakfast for ten people. We spend the morning telling folks where to get kayaks, where to taste wine, how to score dinner reservations. If the cleaning girl doesn't show, I'm in the rooms, seeing things no one should see. At the end of the day, if we're still awake, we can share a glass of wine with each other on our terrace, hiding from the guests."

"But you love it," Olivia said, more a statement than a question. She so idealized her friend's exotic French life that she couldn't imagine otherwise.

"I love it," Emily said wearily.

"We would not want to do anything else," Sébastien said, more sure of himself. "After my mother died I needed to come home to France. Now I have lunch with my father in Marseille every Sunday. I will know when he is sick, when he is dying. I will be with him, not four thousand miles away."

Sébastien and Emily met in business school in Manhattan. Emily wanted to expand her work as an interior designer. Sébastien wanted to learn English and to make money. They spent twenty-one years in New York; he worked on Wall Street and Emily designed the interiors of public spaces. They hated their jobs and only marginally enjoyed their city. When Sébastien's mother died, two years ago, leaving him the inn in Cassis, they quit work, put their house on the market, and booked flights to France, all within the week.

"What did this place look like when you first took over?" Brody asked.

"A disaster," Emily said. "This garden didn't exist. The house was a mess—the additions on each end didn't match the original."

"The pool was cracked and empty," Sébastien added. "A jungle of weeds grew from the bottom."

"An old rusted bicycle lived in the pool!" Emily told them. "And you can't imagine the collections tucked into every corner of the house. Owls. Cuckoo clocks. Wild-eyed dolls."

"My mother was odd," Sébastien summed up.

"Crazy."

"*Oui,*" he said. "*Elle était folle.*"

Sébastien reached out and took Emily's hand. "Emily created this place from nothing. I will show you photos later. You will not believe what she had to work with."

"And Sébastien did most of the work," Emily said proudly. "The guy hasn't put on a suit since we left New York. Now he wears a tool belt. It's much sexier."

"See," Sébastien said, "it is all about *le sexe.*"

Emily rolled her eyes. "If I'd seen this place, I never would have come," she told them. "We spent a full year renovating before we opened the inn. Even now there are three million projects to keep Sébastien busy."

"The caretaker's cottage is next," Sébastien said. "We can rent two more rooms once we finish that."

"You need a hand this weekend?" Brody asked.

"No!" both Emily and Olivia shouted at once. They all laughed.

"No way are you disappearing into guy land," Olivia said. "I need Brody here. At my side."

A bell rang loudly, sending Ulysse into another flurry of barks and yelps.

"C'est qui?" Sébastien asked, looking at Emily.

She shrugged. "No guests this weekend," she said. "That's for sure."

"Someone got here early," Olivia grumbled. "They're going to ruin my one good night."

The bell rang again, more insistently this time.

Sébastien pushed himself up and walked away, sipping from his champagne glass. "I send the person away," he said. *"Je reviens tout de suite."*

"It's probably some tourists who think they can get a room last minute," Emily said.

"Are you booked all the time?" Brody asked.

"Pretty much. It's a blessing and a curse. Success in the first year. I wasn't quite ready."

"You seem to be doing great," Olivia said, but she wasn't sure. Emily looked tired. Of course she's tired—she's running an inn. Olivia watched her as she opened a bottle of white wine. She was still beautiful at fifty-five but her skin was lined, her once blond hair mostly gray. Olivia experienced a time warp whenever they got together. They were supposed to be twenty.

"I am," Emily said. "It's just a lot to take on."

"Can you hire help?" Brody asked.

"I will. For now, this place needs me here. Once we've been in operation for another year I may bring on a manager."

They heard voices, loud voices. A woman was yelling. Sébastien said, *"Non!"* in a voice Olivia had never heard before, an angry, forceful voice. Emily stood and one of the champagne glasses fell to the ground, shattering against the stones.

"Merde," she muttered.

"I'll clean that up," Olivia said. "You go see what's—"

Emily walked over the broken glass and headed down the path.

"Should we go?" Olivia asked Brody.

He shook his head. "Their business. Ours is to sit here and get drunk."

"I should clear away that glass."

"Later," Brody said, reaching for Olivia's hand.

She loved his calm in the face of all drama. He had the power to settle her, to make her believe in love and marriage and partnership.

"Arrête!" Sébastien shouted.

"Sounds bad," Olivia said.

"Probably some privileged tourist who can't imagine that they won't accommodate him tonight."

"How do you know it's a man?"

"I doubt Sébastien would shout at a woman like that."

They heard a crash—another glass breaking? Someone falling? Both Olivia and Brody leapt to their feet. They headed down the path toward the noise.

When they emerged from the garden they saw a woman standing beside Sébastien at the bottom of the drive. The gate for cars was closed, but beside it the door hung open. Emily stood at the top of the drive, watching.

The woman was talking in hushed tones—was she crying?— and then she threw herself at Sébastien, wrapping her arms around him. He pried her off of him, and held her away with his hands on her shoulders.

He said something to her in a low voice, his French too fast and quiet for Olivia to hear. She glanced at Brody and raised her eyebrows. He tilted his head as if to say, Should we get out of here?

"Sébastien?" Emily called. Still, she kept her distance from them.

"*Elle s'en va,*" Sébastien said loudly. "She does not belong here."

The woman was short and curvaceous, wearing a white dress with a thick black belt wrapped around a narrow waist. He's fucking her, Olivia thought. She headed toward her best friend.

Emily stood with her arms across her chest, her back rigid. Her eyes were dark with anger.

"Who is she?" Olivia asked, standing by her side and watching the scene down the hill.

"No fucking clue," Emily said through tight lips.

Sébastien was spitting words at the woman. He looked ready to haul off and punch her.

"Oh my God, she's crying," Emily said. "Spare me."

The woman buried her face in her hands and her shoulders heaved. Sébastien turned her around and marched her out the door.

When he shut the door, he put his head against it and stood there, his back to them. After a moment he turned and walked up the hill wearily. He stopped in front of his wife.

"Ta petite amie?" Emily asked.

Your girlfriend. Olivia's French wasn't as good as Emily's, but she understood enough.

Sébastien looked at his feet.

"Answer me," Emily insisted.

"Non," he told her.

"Cochon," Emily said, and she turned from him. She charged up the hill toward the inn. Olivia followed her, a few steps behind.

She could hear Sébastien call Emily's name, his voice wobbly.

Emily stormed through the door and into her apartment behind the reception area. She closed the door behind her. The lock slammed into place.

When Olivia turned around, Brody was standing in the doorway of the inn, watching.

"What do I do?" she asked.

"Let's get out of here," he said quietly. "We'll get dinner in town."

"I can't leave her," Olivia said.

"This is their rodeo," Brody told her.

He took her hand and led her out of the house. Sébastien was nowhere to be seen. They walked down the hill, and Olivia clung to Brody's hand as if some calamity was ready to strike them. The world felt tilted somehow. At the bottom of the hill, near the gate, they saw the shards of Sébastien's champagne glass scattered over the stones. Olivia bent down and was about to pick up the stem of the glass when Brody tugged on her other hand.

"Leave it," he said, his voice surprisingly strong. "Let them clean up their own mess."

He opened the door and led her away from the inn.

Later that night, after bouillabaisse at a small restaurant on the edge of the harbor, after a long walk through the small cobblestone streets of the old town and then back up the hill to the inn, Olivia and Brody held each other in bed. They were naked, their bodies curled around each other.

"We're brave old fools," Olivia said, her mouth pressed to Brody's ear.

"How's that?" he asked.

"We still choose love when we know everything that can happen," Olivia whispered.

"We still choose love," Brody said, kissing her.

Chapter Two

"Come with me to my mother's wedding," Nell said.

"Whoa," the man said. He was wearing black-framed glasses, the kind of glasses that could be hip or geeky. Nell considered the possibility that they were fake and that he wore them to make himself look a little less handsome. That's absurd, she thought. No one would do that.

"I'm serious," she told him. "We'll have a great time."

He watched her. She kept her gaze firm. They were sitting next to each other on the airplane, their faces uncomfortably close. She could feel herself begin to tremble and she tightened her hand around her plastic cup. He lifted the small bottle of wine off his own tray and poured the rest into her cup.

"I'm Gavin," he said. "Nice to meet you." He tapped his cup against hers.

"We met a few hours ago."

"But I missed the transition to family weddings."

"It's a small wedding. In Cassis."

"All the more reason to invite a stranger," he said.

"You don't feel like a stranger," she lied. She knew the point at which she upped the ante. She had been enjoying herself, chatting up the hot guy beside her on the flight. He flirted, she flirted right back. They drank, told each other stories, he ran his finger along her arm. And then she pushed against her own sense of decorum—no, not decorum—she didn't believe in decorum. She pushed beyond what she imagined any other daring young woman might do. Beyond what even she was comfortable doing. Why? Damn the therapist who asked her that so many times that she finally quit seeing him. Damn her mother who challenged: "What are you waiting for, Nell? For me to tell you that you've gone too far? It's too late for that." Damn her father who just last week said "Grow up, Nell. I don't want to deal with your foolishness anymore."

"So tell me about this wedding," the man said, taking off his glasses and rubbing the bridge of his nose. Gavin. Nice name. Nice blue-gray eyes, the color of slate. He had already told her he was going to explore the south of France. "How?" she had asked. "I'll figure it out when I get there," he had told her. And so she became the woman who might enchant such a man. The woman who would invite him to her mother's wedding.

Now she told him about the man her mother was marrying, the friends who ran the inn, the younger sister from Silicon Valley, the cowboy friend of the groom and the old lady from Wyoming.

"And me," Gavin said.

"And you," she told him.

"The stranger from the airplane."

"The good-looking man in seat 43A who charmed his way into my mother's wedding."

"I'd love to come," he said.

"I'd love you to come," she said.

He leaned forward and kissed her and kept kissing her. A shiver ran through her body. He tasted of wine and coffee. They had been drinking both for hours, not wanting the buzz to fade.

She had done the right thing, she decided, though her mind filled with the voices of so many people telling her to stop, to walk away, to grow up, to set boundaries. She felt his hand on her thigh and knew from the current that ran through her that he would be someone she'd like to take to bed. Her legs opened. He gripped the inside of her thigh a little too hard and something in her chest tightened. He might be dangerous, she thought, and her legs slipped open a little more.

They drove along the coast from Nice, headed west, away from the high-rise apartment buildings and overdeveloped hillsides, away from the autoroute that scared Nell with its fast cars and unintelligible signs. She found the slow road to Cassis, one that hugged the Mediterranean, one that kept them inching slowly toward her family.

She had sobered up. He was still appealing in a rough-around-the-edges way, but now the notion of introducing him to her mother seemed ludicrous. She could lie about when and how they met. But then he would know she was not the daring woman she had presented herself to be. Story of her life: Creating a fantasy and then crashing into it full-force with her own dumb reality. You can't take a total stranger to your mother's wedding.

And you can't fall in love on an airplane.

Who said anything about love? Wasn't she just anticipating one or two wild nights in bed? And then he would go on with his grand adventure, exploring the coast, however the hell he planned on doing that in the first place.

She hadn't slept with anyone since Chaney.

"I fell asleep," he mumbled, stirring, adjusting his glasses, clearing his throat. Then his hand reached out and stroked the back of her neck.

"We should have slept on the plane," she said.

"No," he said. "We were having far too much fun for that."

She smiled. He pressed his fingers into the nape of her neck and she felt a flush course through her body. This will be fine, she told herself. Her mother will be too occupied with everything else to care very much about one extra person at the wedding. One stranger.

"Where are you from?" she asked.

"You're worried about introducing me to your mother."

She shot him a look. Mind reader. He was smiling, a devilish smile.

"Not at all," she said. "My mother has a weakness for good-looking men."

"And you? Do you do this often?"

"Take strange men to my mother's wedding? Not often."

"So now I'm strange."

"Very."

"I'm from Seattle."

He was lying. He wore a black T-shirt and skinny black jeans. He carried a leather bomber jacket and wore black Doc Martens. New York maybe. L.A. This guy was not from Seattle.

"What's wrong?" he asked.

Whoever he was, he could read her shifts in temperature. A good sign.

"Not a thing," she said. "I love Seattle."

She hated Seattle. She hated the rain, the sincerity, everyone's outdoorsiness. She once spent a month in Seattle with a boyfriend and fled the place, leaving her rain gear behind.

A burst of nervous laughter escaped her.

"What's so funny?" he asked.

"What did we talk about for all those hours on the plane? We know nothing about each other."

"Are you worried?"

"No," she said quickly.

"Neither am I," he told her. He placed his hand on her thigh and even through the material of her jeans, she felt as if he was pressing the flesh of his palm into her skin. Her body temperature rose.

She threw the map on his lap. "Help me find Cassis," she said. "We'll tell each other the stories of our lives later on in bed."

"I like that," he said.

He was good at maps. He directed her left and right, through small fishing villages and larger vacation communities. When they were stopped at a light in the center of one town, he jumped out of the car and for a moment she thought:

He's gone. Her heart lurched. She wanted him back and she wanted him gone forever. She wanted to sleep with him and fall in love with him and yet she didn't want to bring him to the damn wedding. And then she conjured the worst of what would happen: her younger sister. Carly—practical, rational, reasonable Carly—would kill her. She pulled to the side of the road, then looked in the backseat. His backpack was there, piled on top of her suitcase. They hadn't been able to open the trunk.

The car door opened again and he climbed in, bearing ice-cream cones. She felt ridiculously happy, like a child, like a lover, like a woman who knew the man behind the cones.

"How did you know I like pistachio?" she asked.

He smiled. His own cone held chocolate ice cream. Had he given her chocolate ice cream she might have sent him on his way. Instead, she had fallen a little deeper. In love? In lust. She was a fool. But at least she was a fool with a cone full of pistachio ice cream.

"It's hot in here," he told her. "I needed to cool off."

The air conditioner was broken. Or was he talking about the heat between them? She pressed her legs together.

She ate her ice cream and watched a mother try to maneuver a double stroller across the busy street, a boy hanging on to her skirt, delinquent dad following a few steps behind, his eyes focused on a cellphone. Through the open car window she could hear one baby wailing, the boy yelling, the mother trying to soothe him.

"That woman is probably my age," Nell said.

"You didn't leave a husband and three kids behind in Los Angeles?" Gavin asked.

"I didn't even leave a job behind."

"A boyfriend?"

She looked at him. He had a smudge of chocolate at the edge of his lip. "Just so you know," she said. "I don't like chocolate ice cream. I love all things chocolate except for ice cream."

"I knew that," he said, smiling.

"And I don't have a boyfriend. The last one killed himself. In our bedroom. I'm still working on the aftermath of that one."

"I'm sorry," Gavin said. "I can't imagine." She saw tenderness on his face, something new, something that made her open her heart a little more.

Good response, Nell thought. She hated the friends who told her it wasn't her fault or the folks who tried to top her with horror stories of bad relationships. It hadn't even been a bad relationship. It had been wonderful, except for the suicide part. Chaney had died six months earlier and she had moved out of the apartment the day she found him lying in bed, bottles of pills—many of them her pills—strewn across the sheets.

"You have a family and kids back home?" she asked.

He shook his head. "Tell me about the boyfriend."

She raised her eyebrows. Brave man. So she told him that she and Chaney had been living together for a year, having met at an audition. Both of them were actors, they read well together, got turned down, went for beers at the nearby pub. She didn't mention that she moved in with him the night they met. Or that she had left behind a different boyfriend, in a fancier apartment, one who waited for her for days to return. She finally moved her things out of the old place when he was at work. She left him a Dear John letter, a pathetic excuse of a note. The old guy—and he was old, forty-five to her twenty-seven—had two kids, a miserable divorce, a high-stress job, a drinking problem. Chaney seemed so easy to her. She felt like a kid again with him, carefree and broke, free to have sex whenever they wanted. Even her mother liked Chaney, especially after she saw him in *True West* at a small L.A. theater. In the weeks before his suicide, he had been called back three times for a breakout role in a film and finally his agent had told him by voice mail that he hadn't gotten the role. He killed himself a few hours later. Had he wanted that role so much that he couldn't live without it?

Maybe she had been missing something while having fun with Chaney. Maybe he wasn't so easy after all.

But she didn't tell Gavin that. She told him about finding out that Chaney was bipolar, something he had never revealed. His mom told her at the funeral. "Oh, I know," she had lied to the woman. "But he was doing so well."

Now she rented a room in someone's broken-down house in Venice. She had a bit part every once in a while in a cop show on TV. She was studying to be a yoga teacher. So was everyone else.

A horn blasted and her hands flew to the steering wheel. She and Gavin were still sitting in the car at the side of the road in some small beach town in France. They had finished their ice-cream cones long before. She reached over and wiped the chocolate at the side of Gavin's mouth.

"Thank you," he said. "For telling me all that."

She nodded. Okay. Time to bring the stranger to the wedding.

"We're here," she said, leaning over and pointing to a spot on the map that sat on the gearshift between them. "This is Cassis. Lead me to my mother."

She pulled back onto the road. Her eyes were tired. She hadn't slept in a day or two. She shifted gears and then hooked a finger under the sleeve of Gavin's T-shirt. She pulled him toward her and felt his mouth on her ear. Soft lips, hot breath. For the first time in a long while she felt something like happiness spread through her.

The gate of La Maison Verte was open. They drove up the hill and turned into a small parking lot. Nell had the familiar feeling of being late, of having screwed something up even before the party began. She felt her breath get shallow—years of acting training and yoga had taught her how to slow her breath but now all that was useless. She was in full-on terror mode. Her mother would kill her.

"You're sure about this?" Gavin asked.

He was pulling his backpack out of the car, throwing it over one shoulder. Where would he be now if she hadn't invited him along? Hitchhiking at the side of the road? He seemed to come from nowhere and to be headed nowhere. And yet he looked so at ease here, so full of confidence and charm.

"I'm very sure about this," she told him. "Let's meet the 'rents."

They walked up the hill toward the inn. They could hear voices coming from the side of the inn—a shout from a man, a splash in a pool, a woman's high laughter.

"Did you pack a swimsuit?" Nell asked.

"I don't need one," Gavin told her.

She imagined a late-night swim with him. She imagined sex in a king-sized bed, a deep sleep in his arms, more sex at sunrise. She imagined a walk in the woods tomorrow morning. A picnic on the beach. She imagined everything but this: her family. A wedding. Her mother's questions.

"Let's do it," she said, taking his hand and leading him toward the noise of the swimmers.

They dropped their bags on the lawn and walked around the perimeter of the inn.

"It's gorgeous," she said quietly. She had seen photos of Emily's inn but nothing prepared her for the lushness of the gardens, the quiet, the sense of a world apart.

They rounded the corner and the pool appeared, in the middle of a meadow surrounded by a riot of wildflowers. They both stopped and Nell could hear Gavin, too, hold his breath for a moment.

"Wow," she finally said.

"Nell!" someone shouted and she saw her mother climb out of the pool, her arms raised as if to hug her from afar. And then Olivia spied the stranger and her brow furrowed as if she were trying to recognize him. She turned, grabbed a white terry robe from the lounge chair and wrapped herself in it.

Nell could hear her saying something to the person in the pool—Brody, she guessed. Nell and Gavin stood there, as if frozen, while Olivia turned and started toward them.

"Your mother," Gavin said quietly.

"Yes."

"A woman with a lot of energy," he whispered as Olivia neared, her face animated, her arms fluttering in the air as if she were already in mid-conversation.

"Yes."

Nell dropped Gavin's hand and stepped toward her mother; they threw their arms around each other.

"Welcome!" Olivia called, though Nell was pressed against her. Was she greeting Gavin? Nell pulled away and looked back, no longer sure that he'd even be there.

"Who is this?" Olivia stage-whispered in Nell's ear.

"This," Nell said, reaching to pull Gavin closer to them, "is Gavin. My date."

"Hello, Gavin," Olivia said, extending her hand. He took it and then held her hand in both of his. "Where did you come from?"

"The airplane," Nell said quickly. "Gavin, this is Olivia. The bride."

"So nice to meet you," Gavin said. He hadn't let go of Olivia's hand.

"Come meet the groom," Olivia said, eyeing Gavin.

He held her gaze and then his hands lifted from hers and a smile spread across his face. "A lucky man, that groom," Gavin said.

Olivia raised one eyebrow at Nell. "Smooth," she said. It wasn't a compliment.

She turned and walked back to the pool, her head high, like the queen of the manor, despite the bathrobe, the bare feet, the wet scrambled hair.

Nell and Gavin followed. She wrapped one arm around his waist and kept him close.

"Nell!" Brody called, emerging from the pool. He grabbed a towel and wrapped it around his waist, then moved toward them, as happy as a groom at his wedding. When Olivia passed him in the other direction she muttered something under her breath, something that Nell couldn't hear.

"Don't mind the water," Brody said, taking Nell in his arms.

She shrieked and cuffed him; he laughed and tousled her hair as she pulled away.

"You're soaking wet!"

"Needed to cool you off," he said, beaming.

She looked down; her blouse was drenched. She groaned. But she liked Brody, had liked him from the start. He was the anti-dad, not that she was looking for another dad. He went easy on her and he seemed to enjoy her tales of wacky life in L.A. Most important, he made her mom happy. Her father had failed on all those accounts. She had no idea what it would mean to have a stepdad but she'd happily give this guy a chance.

Brody offered a hand to Gavin. "I'll get a bottle of rosé to welcome you," he said after they'd exchanged names. "Let's get this party started."

"I'm plotting revenge," Nell said, pulling the towel from Brody's waist, then using it to dry herself off.

Brody headed toward the inn. Olivia called after him, "Two bottles! And tell Emily to join us!"

Olivia had positioned herself at the end of a long wooden table. When Nell and Gavin walked up to join her, Olivia stood and turned to Gavin. "Why don't you give Brody a hand? You can grab glasses for everyone."

"Mom, we just—"

"Go on," Olivia said firmly.

Gavin nodded and headed toward the inn.

Nell slumped into a seat at the table. She put her head in her hands. "I'm exhausted," she moaned.

"Who is he, Nell? Why is he here?"

"Let's start with a few kind words," Nell said, looking at her mom. "Good to see you, Nell. Thanks for coming halfway around the world for my wedding."

"That, too," Olivia said, offering a small smile.

Nell put her hand on her mother's. "You look half your age. You look like a girl on her wedding weekend."

"Enough kind words," Olivia said. "Who the hell is he?"

"He's kind of cute, isn't he?"

"He is."

"And polite."

"Seems to be."

"Oh, God, Mom. Just cut me a break on this one."

"You met him on the airplane and invited him to my wedding."

"Guilty."

"My intimate wedding of closest family and friends."

"He's going to make one member of your closest family a happier person this weekend."

"You couldn't manage that yourself?"

"Mom, it's done. He's here."

Olivia closed her eyes and held them closed. Nell imagined fire spreading through her mother's veins.

"*I'm* here," Nell finally said.

Olivia opened her eyes. She shook her head and then offered a crooked smile. "You are most certainly here."

"Besides, Carly's coming with Mr. Clean. We know Gavin will be far more fun than that guy."

Mr. Clean was Nell's name for Wes, Carly's boyfriend. He was bald and a neat freak, hyperorganized, a little compulsive. No one liked him except for Carly.

"What do you know about Gavin?" Olivia asked.

"They're coming," Nell said, gesturing toward the back door of the inn where the men were exiting, balancing bottles and glasses and bowls in their arms.

"You don't know a thing about him," Olivia said.

"I know I like him," Nell countered.

"Okay. We'll start there." Olivia stood up and reached for a bottle of wine from Brody's arms.

"Emily's working with Paolo," Brody said. "She can't join us."

"Who's Paolo?" Nell asked.

"The chef for the weekend."

"I can help in the kitchen," Gavin said.

"You cook?" both Olivia and Nell said at once.

Nell laughed. "I knew that," she said.

"I love to cook," Gavin told them.

Nell beamed. "See?" she said to her mom.

She pulled a chair close and Gavin sat beside her.

"Where are you from?" Olivia asked him.

"Seattle," Nell said at the same time that Gavin said, "Austin."

"Welcome to our wedding weekend," Olivia said, and her eyes seemed to shine bright with anger.

Olivia stood up, dropped her robe and dove into the pool.

"We'll go get washed up," Nell said.

"Emily will show you to your room," Brody said. "I'll keep the wine on ice."

"Thanks, Brody," Gavin said and he slapped Brody's shoulder as if they were old friends.

Who are you, Nell thought, and what are you doing here?

She followed him back to the inn. She knew that both her mother and Brody were watching them. She slipped her arm through Gavin's, leaned her head on his shoulder as they walked.

"Save me," she whispered.

Gavin ran his fingers lightly over Nell's skin as if he were teasing her, testing her, awakening her senses. Her body felt alive, feverish.

"Don't move," he said when she arched toward him, wanting more of him.

She opened her eyes. He was watching her, perched beside her, his chest lean and hairless. His face was serious as he studied her body.

Good, she thought. She was proud of her body, which was fit from yoga, thin from unemployment. She had once been a body double for a sex scene and the director had told her: That body is made for film.

"I can't keep still," she whispered. "You're killing me." She reached for him.

"Don't move," he said, his voice loud, resonating against the stone walls of the small room.

She fell back on the bed and closed her eyes, caught her breath. She felt a rush of heat through her crotch; her heart pounded, warning her. You don't know him. Her legs inched open, inviting his hand between them.

"My God," she murmured when he touched her. Already

she was wet. She fought against the urge to wrap herself around him. Don't move. It echoed in her head, it kept her flat on her back, it kept her heart pulsing in her skull.

But his fingers ran circles through her pubic hair and she began to lift her hips, to press herself into him.

"Don't move," he whispered, his mouth in her ear. He grabbed her wrists and held them above her head, pinning her down.

Please, she thought.

"Don't say a word."

She could come. She couldn't come. She couldn't move. She wouldn't look at him. He was nowhere and everywhere, one finger inside her, one hand on her neck, the pressure coming from both hands, from thrill and fear, heat and ice. She felt a surge of panic and then a wave of something else—give it up to him.

His finger probed the deep space inside her. His hand slid down to her chest and his palm, flat and wide, pressed her into the mattress. He'll break me in half. And then he pulled his finger out from inside her and ran it against her clitoris, teasing her, thrilling her, his voice in her ear: "Don't move."

She came without moving. It blasted through her body and she felt every pore on her skin break open, every muscle tense and release, heat and ice colliding, breaking her apart from the inside.

"Good girl," he said and he lay down next to her.

Chapter Three

When Carly came downstairs with her suitcase, Wes was on the phone, walking in circles around the dining-room table, his own suitcase on top of the table, open and half packed. Or was it half unpacked?

He wouldn't look at her.

The limo was due in ten minutes.

She poured herself a glass of orange juice and drank it standing in front of the sink, her back to Wes. She could hear the urgency in his voice—his work was always urgent—and she knew, even before he got off the phone, that he was not going to come to France.

God damn him, she thought.

"I'll be there in a half hour," he said into the phone. It was six o'clock in the morning.

She turned to him, steeling herself. She wouldn't argue. It wouldn't change anything. And she wouldn't cry. She hadn't cried in a long time when he canceled a trip.

"I'm sorry," he said. "I have to—"

"Spare me the details," she said.

"You know I'd rather get on a plane with you. Go to France."

He didn't say any more. Because next he would have to say: "Go to your mother's wedding." Her mother hated him and he knew that. He so didn't want to go to her mother's wedding.

"Why did you even pretend?" she asked and cursed herself for asking. Go. Walk out and wait for the limo in front of the house.

"I wasn't pretending. Does this look like a pretend suitcase?"

He would have never half packed. The guy never did anything halfway. Except commit to love.

"Yes," she said.

"Carly."

She shook her head. "I'm taking the newspaper," she told him on the way out. He would be angry about that. He was the only guy she knew who wouldn't read on his iPad. She slammed the door behind her.

Even after hours of flying, hours of sleeping and waking and remembering, Carly hadn't settled herself well enough to face her family. The airline had put an old man in Wes's business-class seat on the plane. The man smelled of cigarettes and something else—rotting fruit? Decay? When he asked where she was going she said, "I don't speak English" in perfect English. He watched movie after movie, drinking gin and tonics until he finally fell asleep, snoring riotously.

Now, in her rental car, she glanced at her Google Maps app and ignored the turn-off for the inn. Instead, she followed the signs to CASSIS CENTRAL, hoping to find the port or at least a good bar.

When she neared the town all signs seemed to point to one parking lot or another. She tucked her rental car into one of them and walked downhill for ten minutes. *Et voilà:* a long stretch of cafés and bars along the marina, all of them with terraces. Her heart lifted for the first time in two days.

She chose a beach restaurant, Le Bada, away from the docks and the crowds of tourists. She sat at a small table and gazed out at the Mediterranean. It was late in the afternoon and the sun was starting to drop behind a set of cliffs to the west. Kayakers headed back from their journeys, weary smiles on their sunburnt faces. On the beach, some sunbathers stretched out on the sand, taking in the last brilliant rays. Carly saw a gray-haired paunchy man surreptitiously taking photographs of a young topless beauty while his wife, beside him, busied herself with an elaborate picnic. Carly wanted to smack the guy.

I need a drink, she thought.

Her mom was marrying a cowboy—no, he wasn't a cowboy. Carly knew that. He had been some kind of veterinarian in Bumfuck, Wyoming. But then he gave it all up to move to San Francisco and live with Olivia. Carly didn't trust him. She didn't know him despite having shared a couple of dinners with him and her newly smitten mother. He was a Wyoming man, a tall hunk of a guy. Carly knew nerds and geeks and men like her father, thinking men. She understood those men even if they made her crazy. Wes made her crazy.

"You're still dreaming that your mother and father will get back together," Wes had said to her when they received the wedding invitation. Couldn't her mother have told her in person, rather than by some moronic e-card with champagne glasses as the subject line?

"I am not," she protested. But the next day, when she gently told her dad that Olivia was getting married, she saw him crumble just a little bit. He was not a man who crumbled.

"Good for her," he said, almost to himself. They were sitting in a restaurant in Woodside; just a few minutes earlier a couple of men had stopped by their table to tell him how much they admired him. He was top dog at Silicon Valley's most powerful law firm. Everyone admired him. Carly's mother admired a cowboy.

"The wedding's in France," Carly said, knowing that, too, would pain her father. He and Olivia used to vacation in Paris often, just the two of them. Carly had always loved the idea of it—her parents wandering the streets of Paris, hand in hand, discovering unknown bistros, hidden parks, quirky museums. They'd show her the photo albums later and Carly would imagine herself as an adult, traveling to Paris with her husband, bringing home Jacadi dresses for her own young daughters.

Why was her mother marrying this guy in France? Why didn't her father show some grit? He must still love her, despite the young women he dated now, stupid women who couldn't hold their own in an argument with him.

Maybe he was tired of arguing.

Carly was tired of the voices in her head, all of them clamoring to make sense of nothing. Marriages end. Someone says I quit. Where was her own grit?

"Oui, mademoiselle?" the waiter said, as if they were in the middle of a conversation.

"Champagne, s'il vous plaît," she requested, surprising herself. She had been pining for a beer. The dancing champagne glasses from that idiotic e-card must have penetrated her psyche. Well, bring on the champagne. She'd find something to celebrate.

The waiter disappeared and a man dropped into the seat across from her.

"Excuse me?" she said, ready to rumble. She hated aggressive men in bars. She wouldn't expect French men to mimic Americans this way.

"You're all grown up," the man said.

"Sébastien!" She was out of her chair in a heartbeat. She threw her arms around him.

"It is you," he said, laughing. "I was sure some French girl was going to punch me."

"I was close!" she said.

He kissed her on both cheeks. "So good to see you, *chérie.*"

When they sat down again, Sébastien called to the waiter, whom he apparently knew, and he used some kind of hand signal that seemed to insure that he would get what she had ordered. Carly loved Sébastien, the sexy Frenchman who had swooped in and taken her mother's best friend away. At least that's how Olivia told the story—it was part of the fairy tale of

Emily's charmed life. First a French husband and then the gift of an inn in the South of France.

"Why are you here?" he asked. "Everyone is waiting for you at the inn!"

"I'll get there soon," she said.

"You are hiding," he suggested.

She nodded. "You found me."

"I won't tell."

"And why aren't *you* at the party?"

"I am in zee doghouse."

She burst out laughing. She saw that he was serious, but his French accent mixed with the American phrase jarred her. Besides, how could Sébastien ever be in the doghouse?

"I don't want to know," she told him. "Let's get drunk."

He shook his head. "I cannot bring you home drunk. Your mother will kill me."

"Why is everyone always so scared of Olivia?"

"You are the one who will make men scared," Sébastien said. "I hear you will run the world one day."

Carly shook her head. "I may run a business in Silicon Valley if I'm lucky. That's a far cry from the world."

"In France we think Silicon Valley does run the world."

"It doesn't," she said. "Believe me. Though many of us are filled with delusional dreams."

Only last weekend she and Wes had argued about that. "We are the new masters of the universe," he told her after the company party ended and a few of them stayed late at the bar.

"It's the geek dream," she told him. "And it will be the downfall of this damn town."

At twenty-six she was already cynical about power in the valley. She understood its allure; she knew its danger. The Stanford business school had been a crash course in the menace of masters of the universe. And then she was hired to work at EyeDate, a start-up that was going to revolutionize the dating world, or so Wes boasted to his groupies. Now Carly was Chief Groupie or VP of Operations, whichever title she wished to use. After six weeks on the job, Wes had told her that she would take over the company one day and did she want to go out for dinner that night? They moved in together a few months later. Everything they did was fast and efficient. Even sex.

"You are too grown-up," Sébastien said, smiling.

"I agree," Carly told him. "This weekend I plan on being completely immature."

"I want to watch that," Sébastien told her.

The waiter set their champagne glasses in front of them, filled Carly's glass, then Sébastien's. Before he left, the waiter said something to Sébastien in rapid-fire French.

"Translate," Carly ordered.

"I told you to study French," Sébastien teased.

"What did he say?"

"He thinks you are very sexy."

"You damn Frenchmen," Carly said, though she felt a jolt of pleasure. "In the States I forget that I even have a body."

"*A la France,*" Sébastien said, lifting his glass.

"To France." They clinked and sipped.

Carly felt her shoulders ease away from her ears. She felt as if she had been holding her breath for days, weeks. In anticipation of Wes bailing on the trip? Or was the trip itself the thing that kept her stomach roiling? Her mother was getting married. Everyone else was full of joy. She felt a little like a spy sent from the warring party.

But she would not report back to her father. "I'm not going to show you one photo or tell you one story," she had promised at that lunch.

"Even if your big sister does something so outrageous that you have to call me and rat her out?"

"I don't rat out my sister!" Carly had argued.

"Every day for twenty-six years," her dad said, smiling. "It's your lifeblood. You'd be lost without it."

And so Carly vowed that she'd be a different kind of sister on this trip. And she wouldn't tell her dad a damn thing.

"Where is your boyfriend?" Sébastien asked.

"In zee doghouse," she told him. They both laughed.

"Your sister brought a boyfriend," Sébastien said.

"Nell doesn't have a boyfriend."

"She does now. Olivia is not happy."

"Mom didn't know? Who is this guy?"

Sébastien shrugged his shoulders. "I am just a simple innkeeper."

"Ha!" Carly had stayed with Sébastien and Emily in Manhattan for a week when she was in grad school. She and Sébastien had spent the evenings arguing about the financial world, the recession, the evils of Wall Street. The guy was smart and savvy, and even if he hated his business, he knew it well.

"When we finish our champagne we will take each other back to the inn," Sébastien said. "I will climb back into zee doghouse and you will climb into the bosom of your family."

"That sounds disgusting," Carly said. Her champagne was gone; she wanted more. She wanted to sit and chat with Sébastien at this table on the edge of the beach all weekend.

"Your mother will be very happy to see you," he said.

It was true. Her mother adored her. For a surprising moment, Carly imagined seeing Olivia at the end of a long expanse of grass, imagined running to her mother as if she were a child and throwing her arms around her. And she knew what she would feel. Love. The full force of unequivocal love.

So what kept her here, ordering another glass of champagne, humoring Sébastien with stories of the tech industry at its wonkiest? Fear, perhaps. Because if it was love she wanted, then what the hell was she doing with Wes?

"Mesdames et messieurs!" Sébastien called out from the doorway of the dining room. "I present the Prodigal Daughter!"

Olivia was the first to leap from her seat, cross the space from table to doorway in a flash, and engulf Carly in an embrace. From over the top of Olivia's head—her mother was five inches shorter than both daughters—Carly caught Nell's eye. Her big sister blew a kiss and smiled beatifically. Happy Nell. That's something new and different, Carly thought. And then she saw the guy, a scrawny hipster dude, though yes, he had some kind of roguish appeal. He kept his eyes on her while she checked him out. No fear in that guy.

"You look wonderful!" Olivia said, pulling back and holding Carly at arm's length. "Where were you? You're hours late! You've never been late once in your life!"

But her mother was smiling, that easy smile spreading across her beautiful face, and when Carly looked around the table she saw that everyone was smiling. It's a cult, she thought. They're all drinking the wedding Kool-Aid.

Then Brody was standing in front of her, and Olivia stepped back as if offering him to her. Don't hug me, please don't hug me, Carly thought.

He leaned forward and kissed her cheek. "I'm so glad you came," he said.

"Of course I came," she told him.

"Where's Wesley?" Olivia asked, and Carly wished he were standing by her side just so her mother wouldn't have the pleasure of hating him more.

"An emergency at work," Carly said.

"Poor you," Olivia offered, reaching out a hand.

Carly bristled. "I'm fine," she said.

"I know you're fine," Olivia said gently. "I'm so glad you're here. You're the only one I can count on who won't turn everything upside down and inside out. Now come to dinner, sweetheart."

Carly walked around the table, greeting Emily, Nell, Mystery Man, an older woman who turned out to be Brody's mother and a sunburnt, windswept guy named Jake, who introduced himself as the best man. She fell into a chair between Emily and Jake, until Nell protested that she was too far away, prompting a shifting of seats so that she landed next to her sister at the end of the table.

"Pour this girl some wine!" Nell called, and five bottles got passed their way. Everyone was well on their way to drunk. Good, Carly thought. No one will notice her own wobbly state.

Now she was across from Emily, who looked nothing like

her usual lovely self. She seemed sleepy and unkempt, as if she had forgotten to change from her work clothes to party mode. Emily had always played second mom to Carly, especially during her teenage years. Carly admired Emily's focus on work, her calm manner, her ability to listen, all things she faulted her own mother for lacking. And now that she was in her twenties, she sometimes turned to Emily as a friend rather than a mom substitute. Easier to talk to Emily about her work-obsessed boyfriend than Olivia, who would just repeat the same mantra: "Get out. You deserve better."

How did Olivia know what Carly deserved? Maybe Wes was exactly what she deserved since she, too, seemed incapable of much more than cohabitation. Wasn't she just as ambitious as Wes, just as distracted when it came to matters of the heart? Love? She always thought she loved Wes but maybe she just admired him. Does admiration have anything to do with love?

Carly whispered across the table to Emily. "You okay?"

Emily shrugged. Carly remembered zee doghouse. Sébastien sat at the other end of the table and was already deep in conversation with the best man, whoever the hell he was.

"A toast," Olivia called out.

"Another?" Nell groaned.

"This will be a weekend of toasts!" Olivia announced cheerfully. "I'd like to raise a glass to my wonderful daughters. Last night I was ready to elope. Now, seeing you both at this table in this enchanting inn, I can't imagine any other kind of wedding. To Nell and Carly!"

"To Nell and Carly!" everyone shouted. And then there was a cacophony of clinks as the many glasses reached out across the table.

Carly sipped her wine. She looked at Olivia and Brody in the center of the large table and thought: Be a sport, girl. It's a goddamn wedding.

Nell threw her arm around Carly. "Where's Mr. Clean?" she asked.

Carly stiffened. She hated the nickname, the delight that Nell, too, would take in Wes's disappearing act.

"He broke his leg last week," Carly said.

"What? How?"

"Skydiving."

Carly felt a moment of panic—she never lied. But with the panic came a delicious rush—she loved the shock on her sister's face. Is this what she meant when she said to Sébastien that she planned on being completely immature this weekend?

"Wes skydives?" Nell asked.

"He loves it. And he's really good at it. There was a freak change in wind."

"That's awful." Nell leaned toward her, those kohl-rimmed saucer eyes filled to the brim with concern. "Did you see it happen?"

"I thought he was dead. You can't even imagine how terrifying it was."

"How bad a break?"

"Really bad. He's had a rough time of it."

"I wish you had called me," Nell said. "I would have come up to help out."

Carly couldn't imagine it—the world takes care of Nell, not the other way around—but she felt a gut-punch of pleasure at Nell's offer.

She remembered her good-sister vow.

"Thanks," she said, putting her arm around Nell. "It just happened. It's been a crazy week."

"Will he be okay?" Nell asked.

"I think so," Carly said. "Tell me about the new beau."

"Later," Nell whispered.

"You're happy," Carly said.

"Yeah," Nell said, and she looked surprised. "I haven't been happy in a long time."

"Good for you," Carly said. She thought about Nell's old boyfriend and the mess of her sister's life after his suicide. Maybe this was something real, this fellow with the two-day beard and the slippery smile. Maybe Nell could find someone who wasn't old or a loser or a drug addict. Give her a chance, the new Carly told the old Carly. She deserves a chance.

"How long have you known him?" she asked.

"Since Flight 97 from New York to Nice."

"Come on."

"Seatmate," Nell said proudly. "And don't say another word. Don't judge me. Just be happy for me."

Carly swallowed all of her words: You're crazy. Who the hell is he? How could you do this to Mom on her wedding weekend? Of course you're happy. You probably just joined the Mile High Club.

"You're about to explode," Nell said, laughing. "Drink up."

Carly took a long gulp of wine. No words slipped from her lips. Perhaps a good sister is a drunk sister, she thought.

Across from her, Emily stood up and began clearing dishes. When Carly tried to help, Emily shook her head. "Sit down, you. You just got here. Eat your first course while the rest of us pause for a second."

Suddenly exhausted, Carly dropped back into her seat. She
was ravenous. She had skipped the airline meals and couldn't
remember the last time she'd eaten. At the other side of the
table, Brody was telling some long story about his best man
bedding two sisters at the same time and everyone laughed
along with him. Beside her, Nell and Mystery Man cooed to
each other. While Carly ate the mussel salad, she watched
Emily and Sébastien pass each other by, moving from the table
to the kitchen, clearing dishes. They never looked at each
other. At one point Emily lowered her head and stepped aside,
giving her husband a wide berth. Trouble in paradise.

New love and old love. Good love and lousy love. And
somehow, I'm all alone, Carly thought.

Hours later they were still at dinner, still drinking wine, still telling stories. Carly needed to escape. She was tired of mingling.
They had been playing a sort of musical chairs, so that every
hour or so she found herself sitting next to different people.

Jake, the best man, was wiry and weathered, as if he'd just
climbed off his horse and roped it up outside the inn. He told
Carly about growing up with Brody in some small mountain
town, both of them living on ranches, getting into trouble with
girls. Brody betrayed him and got married but Jake had always
been a wandering man. Carly felt as if she were listening to the
twangy words of a country song. And she felt the heat of his
dark-eyed gaze; this was a man who liked a conquest. My God,
he was about twenty-five years older than she was. Sorry, cowboy: not interested.

Fanny, mother of Brody, was tall and thin, with white hair
pulled back in a bun. "I'm glad to see my son getting married

again," she told Carly. "One shouldn't grow old alone. It's hard to face the challenges of aging. Good to have a partner when that time comes." And then she turned to her side as if expecting her husband to appear. But it was only Sébastien who sat there, turned away from her. Fanny's face clouded and she seemed lost in thought for a moment. "My Sam left me. Out of the blue. I have to keep reminding myself of that. Fifty-five years with a man and then he's gone." She shook her head, as if ridding herself of him. "Do you have a beau, young lady?"

"Yes," Carly said.

"Is he a man you can grow old with?"

"I'm not sure," Carly told her. She never thought of growing old. Even her mother seemed young to her, despite new wrinkles around her eyes, smile lines indented on her face.

"Find out," Fanny said. "You want a man made of tough stuff."

Wes was made of intellect and inspiration. When Carly tried to conjure him up in her mind she heard words, long strings of sentences that he might say, but she could barely even imagine his face, his body. Tough stuff? Ideas swarm, ignite, dissipate, fly away.

Soon the seats shifted. The candles on the long wooden table flickered. The food appeared and disappeared, the wine-glasses emptied and filled.

Carly never ended up next to Mystery Man. She wondered if he made sure it happened that way. Was he scared of her? He didn't look like he'd be scared of anyone. But she had the feeling that he was playing some kind of role and if she had five minutes with him, she'd be able to pull off the mask. Maybe she'd get the opportunity later. Right now, she didn't care. She was exhausted.

She slipped out of her chair, wineglass in hand, walked halfway around the table and pushed through a door that she thought would lead into the hallway. Instead she walked into the kitchen and almost collided with the chef. He juggled a tray of dessert bowls—filled with some kind of fruit and cream—and when they settled, unspilled, he gave her a wary look.

"Sorry," she said.

But he just watched her. He was young—her age, she guessed. He had a long nose and high cheekbones—too many angles on a thin face. His eyes were the color of a mountain lake.

"You must be the chef," Carly said, inanely. Of course he was the chef.

Still, he didn't answer.

"Do you speak English?" she asked.

"Yes," he said. He hadn't stopped staring at her.

"Go ahead," she said, gesturing at the door.

She held the door open for him and he passed through, tray held high.

The kitchen was all white and wood—a big, airy space that smelled wonderful. Basil, garlic, oregano. Something sweet, too. Vanilla. Carly perched on a stool at the center island.

The chef swung back through the door. He stopped and stared again.

"Is it okay if I sit here? Just for a little while?"

He nodded. Finally, she saw a hint of a smile.

"I am Paolo," he said, the English words strange in his mouth.

"I'm Carly," she told him, offering her hand.

His hand was warm and when he took it away she smelled blackberries.

"Why?" he asked.

She looked at him, confused. He pointed to her stool.

"Too many people in there," she explained.

He nodded.

"Do you understand English?" she asked.

"A little. I understand you."

His mouth seemed to work its way around the English words. And then he smiled, a broad smile that changed his face. She had thought he was unattractive at first—but the smile softened all his edges.

She brought her wineglass to her lips, but it was empty. He lifted an open bottle from the counter and filled her glass.

"Merci," she said, taking a sip.

"Say *grazie*," he said. "I am Italian."

"*Grazie.*" She didn't speak Italian beyond a few words. At least *grazie* was one of them.

She pointed to an empty wineglass on the counter. "For you?"

He filled it and took a sip. "You are bride?" he asked.

She laughed. "No. My mother is the bride."

"Your mother?"

"Second marriage. She's the beautiful redhead out there. She's marrying a cowboy."

"You are not married," he said.

"That is correct."

"You are American?"

"Yes. I'm from California."

"I like San Francisco," Paolo said eagerly.

"I live near there," she told him. "Where do you live?"

"Cassis. But I am from a town near Napoli. Now I live here and work in restaurant."

"You're good," Carly said. "Really good." She had eaten every course—curried mussel salad, tomato and burrata, a pasta dish with chanterelles, sole meunière. So this was the man who had created each perfect dish.

"*Grazie*."

"*Grazie*," she repeated.

"You will eat your dessert here?" he asked.

"Good idea. Will you join me?"

"*Sì*. I join you."

He took two bowls of blackberries, peaches, and cream and placed them on the center island. Then he grabbed a couple of spoons and napkins and sat on the stool next to Carly. He was still wearing his apron, over jeans and a white T-shirt. His hair, wavy and long, was pulled back into a ponytail.

"My sister brought a guy she just met to our mother's wedding," she said, and he raised his eyebrows.

"That is bad?"

"I'm not sure," Carly said. "She's pretty happy."

"She is girl with very short hair?"

"Yes." Nell had cut her hair pixie-style six months ago. Everyone loved it except for Carly who thought it made her look punk rather than gamine.

"She is very pretty, too," Paolo said.

"Say your name for me?" Carly asked.

"Paolo."

"Paolo," she repeated.

He shook his head. "Paolo," correcting her pronunciation.

"I'll get it right the next time," she said, and he smiled.

"Good," he told her.

Chapter Four

Olivia slipped out of her bathrobe and stepped into the pool.

"It's still warm," she said quietly, and then she dove underwater. She swam the length of the pool to loosen up, stretching her arms for a strong crawl. When she touched the wall she turned and swam back.

"Come in," she said, placing her hands on Brody's feet.

He dropped his robe beside hers and dove into the pool. They were both naked in the dark night—even the moon didn't penetrate the clouds. It was two in the morning. Neither of them could sleep.

"That feels great," Brody said, emerging at the other end of the pool.

"Shhh," Olivia said, swimming toward him. "We don't want company."

They both looked toward the inn. All the windows were
dark. Even Ulysse, who eyed them wearily at the back door,
had been too tired to follow them out to the pool. The night air
was filled with the scent of lavender.

"That's the good thing about being in our fifties," Brody
said. "No one's really dying to see us naked anymore."

"They don't know what they're missing." Olivia wrapped
her arms around Brody's waist. "Are you happy to be here?"
she asked, pulling him to her.

"Yes," he said. "Very."

"Your mother seems to be doing all right."

"She puts on a good front. Wyoming stoicism and all that."

"Poor thing."

Brody leaned over and kissed the side of Olivia's head.

"I can't imagine losing you after a year," she said. "Imagine
fifty-five years."

"Of a good marriage," Brody added.

Olivia looked at him, his face lit by the moon now spreading light through the thinning clouds. She reached up and
touched his face.

"I want to grow old with you."

"Let's stay young instead," he said, taking her hand in his.

She thought of his mother, alone in her room at the inn.
Sam should be here, sleeping at her side. Wes should be here,
sleeping at Carly's side. Sébastien should be sleeping at Emily's side, instead of in the pool house, where she saw him slink
off after the dishes were done. Love gone awry.

"There's one thing I want to be sure of," Olivia said.

"What's that?"

"Let's not lose this. Us. In the middle of all the commotion, let's stay just this close."

"And naked?"

"Very naked."

"I like this," Brody said. "It does feel as if we're the only ones here."

"What did you do for your first wedding?" Olivia asked. As soon as the words escaped her mouth, she wanted to retract them. Verboten territory. Do Not Enter.

"This isn't the time," Brody said, releasing her hand. Already his voice was different, as if he were talking to a woman he didn't like very much.

"I'm curious," Olivia said. "That's all. You never told me about your wedding."

She couldn't stop herself. It would be so much smarter to change the subject. But there was something so unreasonable about Brody's refusal to talk about his first marriage. After all, she talked about her disaster of a marriage all the time.

But that's just it. His marriage wasn't a disaster. It was wonderful. It was perfect. And then his wife died.

No way Olivia could ever compete with a dead woman.

But who said anything about competing? Grace was dead. Brody was in love with Olivia now. So why couldn't she let dead wives turn to dust in their graves?

"Do we have to do this?" Brody said, interrupting the jagged twists and turns of her mind.

"Just tell me. Now that I have it in my mind I won't be able to let go of it."

"Why?" Brody asked, truly baffled. "Why do you do this?"

He pushed off against the wall and swam to the shallow end, his strokes hard and fast. Then he sat on the steps and looked at her across the pool. He seemed defeated.

"I'm sorry," she said to him.

He didn't answer.

She swam toward him. She was scared he'd leave before she got there—she kept her head above water and her eyes on him as if fixing him to the spot. When she reached the shallow end, she sat by his side.

"We got married at my parents' ranch," he said quietly.

Of course they did. She felt a pang of jealousy—she imagined a tent in the pasture, line dancing, a bride in a white gown and cowboy boots.

"Was the weather perfect?" she asked, torturing herself.

"It was a hundred degrees," he told her.

"Good."

He put his arm around her. "You dope. Do you also wish I were a virgin?"

"Not that."

He leaned over and kissed her head. Ghosts, she thought. We bring them with us into our new world. They're always out there, hovering close by, ready to join the party at a moment's notice.

"You're shivering," Brody said.

"We'll go in soon," she said.

Olivia heard an owl hooting and then the night was silent again. She needed to let Grace go. Brody had been married to her for fifteen years before she was diagnosed with an aggressive form of breast cancer. She suffered for a year and then died. When Olivia met Brody, two years after Grace's death, he was a bear in hibernation. Big, brooding, a little sleepy, slow to answer her questions. One of his friends, who worked with him at the veterinary hospital, told Olivia, "Have patience. He's still grieving. He's barely reentered the land of the living."

I'll bring him back, Olivia thought then. There was something that drew her to his sorrow, his dark moods. She'd never liked sad sacks, but Brody was different. He was wounded, deeply, and she felt a powerful urge to help him heal.

At first her desires were simple: She wanted to see him smile. She wanted to hear him laugh. She wanted him to stay for a glass of cognac after dinner. Soon enough, she wanted him in her bed. And then she wanted him in her life.

Over the first months, while they traveled back and forth to see each other, he lightened—he looked better, moved faster, no longer fell into long silences. She had feared at one point that she had fallen for a sad man and couldn't love his happy twin. But this was a gift, a discovery. The stronger he got the more she loved him.

"Someone's awake," Brody said, pointing toward the windows on the second floor of the inn.

Olivia couldn't see anything beyond the sheer drapes, but a halo of light brightened a corner of one room.

"Carly?" Brody guessed.

"I bet," Olivia said. "She seems unsettled."

"Her boyfriend bailed."

"There's something else. She seems brittle, breakable."

"Carly? Carly isn't the breaking kind."

"That's why I'm worried," Olivia said. "I always had a rule. Only one kid in crisis at a time. The rule didn't serve them well since Nell was always in crisis. Could be that Carly needs her own meltdown."

"I don't think she'd allow herself one. She's got your strength. I've never seen you fall apart."

"Tomorrow," Olivia said. "Tomorrow's my meltdown day."

"Whew. At least it's not our wedding day."

"Swim with me," Olivia said.

They swam side by side, slowly, back and forth across the length of the pool. Olivia could feel her mind settle with each stroke. Water, darkness, and Brody—all were good for her soul.

"Wait—I hear something," she said, just as they were about to start another lap.

They leaned back against the wall of the pool, trying to quiet their breath. Sure enough, a keening sound penetrated the night.

"Oh my God," Olivia said. "Someone's having sex."

"Not Emily and Sébastien," Brody said. "Emily won't even look in his direction."

The voice—definitely female—cried out and then was silent.

"Nell," Olivia and Brody both said at once.

"I so don't want to hear my daughter going at it."

And then a wail erupted from the inn. The sound reverberated in the dark night.

"Spare me," Olivia said, laughing.

"Shhh," Brody said. They could see someone move to the window. A man, naked, silhouetted by the lamp behind him.

They both dropped underwater and their laughter escaped in bubbles, lifting to the surface of the pool.

When Olivia came up for air, the man was no longer standing in the window. Brody's head emerged in front of her.

"What's his name again?" she whispered.

"Gavin."

"I hate him."

"Why?"

"He'll break my daughter's heart."

"You don't know that."

"I do. Mothers know these things."

"I bet we'll be throwing them a wedding a year from now."

"Impossible. He's too sure of himself. She's not sure of
anything."

"Maybe she's getting stronger. It's been six months."

Olivia had driven down to L.A. when Chaney killed himself. She booked a room for a week at a small hotel on Ocean
Avenue in Santa Monica and deposited Nell onto one of the
twin beds. Nell slept. Olivia spent most of her days perched on
the other bed, making calls to her theater manager, to her director, to the Rainier Theater in Tacoma where they were
scheduled to open with a touring production the following
week. Nell slept through the phone calls, the room-service
meals, the constant calls from Chaney's mother.

Olivia dragged Nell out of bed for the funeral. They sat in the
front of a Baptist church—the mother's church, not Chaney's—
and listened to a long string of eulogies that seemed to have nothing to do with the young man either of them knew. He was
complicated, he was dark, he was ambitious. Chaney? Chaney
was Nell's twin, a sidekick in the game of life. They went to dive
bars and played pool. They took camping trips on weekends and

blew off auditions if the weather was great and they didn't feel like leaving the wilderness. They wrote a screenplay about a mutant housewife who took over the world and they took meetings with Hollywood execs where they talked very seriously about the motivation for their antihero named Wackjob.

After the funeral Nell's mood changed from miserable to angry. She spent one more day at the hotel, tucked under the duvet, but no longer sleeping. She raged against Chaney. Why didn't he tell me? She raged against herself. Why didn't I know him?

Olivia felt safer leaving the angry Nell alone in L.A. Besides, she had to fly to Tacoma to settle an argument between her director and her lead actress. So the next day she helped Nell move into a house in Venice, a well-located firetrap a half block from the beach. She warned her daughter to make sense of this experience before she fell into bed with the next guy. "Sometimes I hate you," Nell had said. But they held each other for a long time before Olivia pushed back, wiped tears from Nell's eyes, and said her goodbye.

Now, six months later, her daughter was hooting and hollering with a stranger in the middle of the night.

"Look," Olivia said, pointing to the second floor of the inn.

Both Nell and Gavin stood in the open window. They kissed for a moment and when they stopped, Nell walked away. Gavin looked out and Olivia was sure that he could see her—that he looked right at her—and then he pulled the window closed. The light went out.

Chapter Five

Nell stroked Gavin's leg as she lay stretched beside him, both of them turned upside down in bed.

"I liked that better," she said.

"Better than what?" he asked.

Their voices were hushed. It was sometime in the middle of the night. Everyone else in the inn was sound asleep. A half hour ago, standing by the window, Nell had said, "Let's go for a swim."

"I'm not done with you yet," he had whispered, taking her back to bed.

But this time he was gentle with her. They made love as if they were lovers, she thought. Tenderly, sweetly.

I could love this man, she thought.

"I liked this version of sex better than round one," she now said, curling into him. "When you held me down. I don't know. It was scary and sexy. But that's not my kind of thing."

"It seemed like your kind of thing."

Other lovers had tried S&M with her, tying her to the bedpost, teasing her with a feather. One boyfriend showed up with a doctor's bag of toys. But it was all playacting and none of it really stirred Nell. Gavin didn't seem to be playing a role when he treated her that way in bed. And yes, she had a very real physical response to his demands.

But now he played a different role. He murmured sweet things while he touched her. He moved with her, letting his own body match her rhythm. He asked her to keep her eyes open so they could watch each other. And that, too, made her want him with a fervor that surprised her. She came easily, but this time, instead of exploding, she felt herself melt into him.

She leaned up and looked at him. His hair fell over his eyes and his face looked soft with sleep. He looked younger than she had guessed on the plane.

"How old are you?" she asked.

"Why?"

"Curious."

"Does it matter?"

"Are you jailbait?"

He gave a half smile, a smirk really, and she wondered if he could be twenty instead of thirty. His body was so thin and sinewy—like a teenage boy. Weird. Could he be that young?

As if he knew what she was thinking, he pushed his hair off of his face and leaned up on one elbow to look at her. In an instant he was older—much older. Could he be forty? His skin looked weathered as if he lived in the sun, doing some kind of hard labor. Jail, she thought. Not jailbait. He had done time. For something. It was in his voice when he commanded her not to move.

Odd, but even this—the thought that he might be an ex-con—didn't scare her. Had sweet sex softened the hard edges of this man?

"I like lying here with you," she said, stroking his back. "I want to know who you are."

His fingers ran through her short hair and then in an instant he made a fist, grabbing her hair at the roots and holding firm. She gasped.

"This is who I am," he said, his voice low. Then he released her hair and stroked her face. "This is who I am," he repeated, his voice a whisper.

She felt herself stir again. Did she like the mystery of him? Did she want to solve him or to keep him unknowable?

"I'm scared of the first version of you," she said. "And I'm scared I'll fall for the second version."

"Don't fall for me," he said quickly. "I'm going to disappoint you."

"Why?"

"It's what I do. It's why I'm on the road all the time."

"No Seattle," she said.

"No Seattle," he told her.

Her hand moved gently over his body; she couldn't stop touching him. His long thighs. His beautiful hands. His hairless chest. Their voices as soft as the night air.

"Tell me about your sister," he said.

"Carly?" Nell pushed herself up and turned around in bed. Gavin followed her and they rearranged themselves, their heads on the pillows, side by side, looking up at the ceiling.

"She's very different from you," he said.

"Yeah." Nell laughed. "I could use some of what she's got. She could use some of what I've got."

"She's never picked up a guy on an airplane," Gavin said.

"Never. I can promise you that."

"She has a boyfriend?"

"He's not good enough for her." And then she remembered his skydiving accident. Poor Wes!

"You love your sister."

"I do. And she makes me nuts."

She turned toward him and saw his smile.

"Do you have siblings?" she asked.

He shook his head. It didn't matter. He could say he had seven brothers or a twin sister and either would be a lie.

"Has your sister ever had a boyfriend who was good enough for her?" he asked.

Nell put her palm on his chest. She could feel the beat of his heart.

"No," she said. "Why?"

"I'm just getting to know you," he said.

No, she thought. You're getting to know my sister. She pushed the thought away.

"This is nice," she said. "Talking like this. I don't think I'll ever sleep again."

He put his hand on top of hers, pressing her hand into his chest.

"I want this," Nell murmured. "I want you."

"You want so much more than that," he said.

"Now I'm scaring you," she said, smiling.

"I'm not scared," he told her. "I know what will happen."

"It might not," she said. "You might decide to give love a chance."

He laughed. "You're very sweet."

She reached over and kissed him. "We could have a good time together," she said.

"Shh," he said. "You talk too much."

He turned her around and wrapped his arms around her. She could hear his breath slow; she could feel his heart pulse against her back. It's so easy, she thought, to be with a man. It's so hard to be alone.

She fell into a dreamless sleep.

Chapter Six

"They've been fucking all night," Carly said into the phone. "I can't sleep."

Carly was lying in bed, her cellphone tucked by her ear. It was two-thirty in the morning—five-thirty in the afternoon, California time. Wes had been surprised by her call. "I thought you were done with me," he had said. "I might be," she told him. "You're the only one I could think of to call at this hour."

The minute she said it, she regretted it. He always gave her a hard time about not having friends. "*You* don't have friends," she would counter. "I'm a guy," he'd tell her. "Guys just need buddies for sports. We don't need to talk to anyone about where to get a manicure."

She knew where to get a manicure. She didn't have girl problems that needed a call-out to five sorority sisters to meet for cosmos and Kleenex. She had Wes and they talked the same language. She didn't need to learn girl talk to feel better about herself.

She stretched her legs above her. Her muscles tensed and then eased. She had stopped playing tennis when she went to Stanford. Maybe she'd join a league again when she returned to California. Maybe she'd work less. Maybe she'd leave Wes.

She remembered her lie about his broken leg and felt a pang of guilt. What's wrong with me, she thought.

No wonder she couldn't sleep. She couldn't turn off her mind. When Carly was little her mother would come into her bedroom and turn an imaginary key on her forehead. "Now go to sleep," Olivia would whisper. How did she know that Carly's mind churned for hours on end? Sometimes even now, in her twenties, Carly would turn the key on her own forehead, hoping that she'd fall into an easy sleep.

"Who is this guy?" Wes asked. "Nell's bedmate?"

Wes had told her he was between meetings. She guessed that he was itching to hang up, to get to the next meeting, but his guilt kept him captive on the phone. Or was it his fear? Was he scared she'd leave him? Was she scared to leave him? How did people manage relationships when love doesn't fit any algorithm that she could define?

"Who knows? A pickup. A one-nighter. Who the hell knows?"

"You sound exhausted."

"I don't really want your sympathy," Carly said.

"I give you everything you want," Wes said, his voice tender in her ear.

"You do?" she asked. "That's all you've got?"

"It's all you ask for."

"What's that supposed to mean?"

"It's too late to have this conversation," Wes said wearily.

"Too late at night or too late in our relationship?"

Wes laughed lightly. "Both," he said.

Carly rolled herself to a seated position. The walls were quiet—finally. Perhaps the lovebirds were sleeping. Didn't matter now. She was wired.

She got up and moved to the window, the cellphone still at her ear though neither of them was talking. At first she could only see the black silhouette of the hills, set against an even darker sky. Soon her eyes adjusted and she could see the swimming pool, and in it, two swimmers, their bodies naked.

She stepped back as if they could spot her. But no, they were doing laps, side by side, their bodies reflected in the sudden moonlight. She looked up at the sky—the clouds had parted and stars appeared, more stars than she thought possible.

"My mother and Brody are skinny-dipping," she whispered into the phone.

"At two-thirty in the morning?" Wes asked.

"It's like a party here but no one knows that I've been invited."

"Because they don't know you're watching?"

"They're not having sex. They're just swimming."

"I know, Carly," Wes said, his voice strained. "I didn't understand what you said. About not being invited to the party."

"Nothing," Carly said, impatiently. "First I have to listen to Nell. And now I have to watch this."

"Close the window. Go back to bed."

But she stood there, transfixed. It seemed so easy for them, matching their strokes, both of them loose and languid in the water. Brody was so much taller and stronger than her mom but he swam at her side. Was Olivia faster—well, her mother was always faster than everyone else—or did he slow his pace to align himself with her? Is that what partners did? She remembered Christmas in Maui with Wes. Her first day there she called the tennis center and asked them to set her up with a good match, someone who played at a 4.0 level. When she got off the phone Wes was staring at her, his mouth hanging open.

"Really?" he asked. "We finally take a vacation and you're going to play tennis with someone else?"

He wasn't a good enough tennis player—that was the reason she had looked for a better game. Was she wrong? Should she have put herself on the other side of the net, watching him struggle to return her forehand smashes? Apparently, the answer was yes. She knew that now because Wes tested everyone they knew with this scenario. They all laughed and rolled their eyes: Yes, Carly was not a very good girlfriend. Yes, Carly preferred a good workout to love on the tennis court.

Brody and Olivia stopped swimming and sat on the steps in the shallow end. At least their bodies were underwater—Carly didn't want to see them naked. Her mother was still fit for a fifty-five year old—and she figured Brody was probably buff, cowboy that he was—but she didn't want to think about her mother and sex.

"Are you still there?" Wes asked into the silence.

Carly stepped back from the open window.

"Yes. I'm here."

"I'm sorry I'm not there with you," he said.

"No, you're not."

"Okay, I'm sorry I'm not anywhere else in France with you. You're right that I didn't want to go to your mother's wedding."

"It doesn't matter what you want," Carly said, and to her surprise she found herself fighting back tears. "You should have done this for me."

Wes was quiet for a moment. "I'm sorry," he said softly.

"Yeah, me, too," Carly said.

Still neither of them hung up. Carly knew that the minute she said goodbye she'd be alone at a wedding in Cassis. She pressed the phone to her ear and listened to the silence.

Chapter Seven

Olivia stretched her hand out across the bed—Brody, I need Brody. She reached for him through the hazy swirl of a dream. Her hand rested on the warm spot where he had slept. Where was he? She looked around. Early morning light, tangled sheets at her feet, the drapes lifting with the wind as if they, too, were haunted.

"Brody?" she called out.

Saturday. She tried to recall what was planned for this day. Kayaking in the calanques, whatever they were. Brody had set it all up and she had agreed, though right now she imagined sending the guests away so she and Brody could spend the day in bed.

He'd never agree to that. The man loved an adventure. So

did she, but not one that included boatloads of people. Her people.

Where was Brody?

The bathroom door was open—no one in there. She leaned over the edge of the bed and scanned the floor. His running shoes were gone—the guy had headed out for an early morning run. Good for him, she thought.

She pushed herself out of bed and shuffled into the bathroom. Squinting at herself in the mirror, she saw everything she didn't want to see. Wrinkles, dark circles under her eyes, weariness. In her mind she didn't look like that woman in the mirror. She still felt like a kid, like someone not quite ready for the grown-up world. But she had managed to raise two girls who were now adults, of sorts, and she had finally snagged a great guy. Adulthood should be wondrous. Was it? Aging sucked. She turned away from the mirror.

Someone was tapping on the door. She threw on Brody's boxer shorts and his T-shirt, deep-breathing his musky scent. "Coming," she mumbled.

She threw open the door and released a happy sigh. Emily. The only person she really wanted to see other than Brody.

"Aren't you supposed to be wearing a sexy negligée on your wedding weekend?" Emily asked, eyeing Olivia's outfit.

"This is as sexy as it gets," Olivia told her.

"Your hunk went running," Emily said. "You want breakfast?"

"Only if you promise that it's just us. I'm not ready for the multitudes."

"I promise," Emily said.

Olivia walked out barefoot and shut the door behind her.

She wrapped her arm through Emily's and they headed down the hallway.

"You doing okay?" Olivia asked.

"Shh," Emily warned. "We want them all to stay asleep."

"Right, boss," Olivia whispered. But she wondered if Emily *would* talk about Sébastien. Emily was private. She didn't ever mention marital problems so Olivia assumed there weren't any. Who doesn't have marital problems? And Olivia hadn't even known that Emily hated New York until she announced her move to France. Emily was Olivia's counsel through her taking over the theater company, through her divorce, through every kid problem that lasted more than a week, but Olivia rarely heard about the inner workings of her best friend's life.

They made their way downstairs and into the kitchen. Early-morning light streamed through the many windows of the room and Olivia felt her bones settle in her body.

"Do I need a graduate degree to work that thing?" she asked, pointing at the mammoth espresso maker on one counter.

"I've got it," Emily said. "Sit here."

She offered a stool at the center island, one that faced the large windows and a beautiful view of the garden and the vineyards beyond.

"You wake up like this every morning," Olivia said, sitting and sighing.

"And ten minutes later I've got an earful of noise from guests demanding a tour and tasting at the best winery in Bandol."

"Oh, yeah, the guests," Olivia said. "I hear you."

The espresso maker silenced them for a minute and the smell of freshly ground coffee filled the room.

"Thank you for this," Olivia said when Emily sat beside her, placing two cups in front of them.

"The espresso's easy," Emily said.

"Giving us your inn for a weekend isn't so easy."

"It would have been if—if Sébastien hadn't ruined everything." Emily reached for a notebook and started leafing through the pages.

"He might have ruined your weekend. But he's not going to ruin ours."

Emily nodded. She flipped pages of the notebook. Olivia saw sketches of food.

"Did you hear me?"

"You think he just ruined my weekend?" Emily asked, a sharp edge in her voice. Finally she looked at Olivia, her eyes hard.

"I didn't mean that," Olivia said. "I know what he did was awful. I know how deep a wound that must be."

"Do you?" Emily asked.

"I can imagine," Olivia assured her. "Em. This isn't about me. I'm just trying to be here for you."

Emily slammed the notebook shut. "I don't know what Paolo's thinking. He can't make crème brûlée tonight. It's his worst dessert. He burns it every time."

Olivia reached out and touched Emily's shoulder. Emily flinched.

"Em. Talk to me."

Emily dropped her head to the table and covered it with her arms. Olivia rested her hand on her friend's lower back.

"It's not your fault. I'm just in a rage."

"I've never seen you in a rage."

"I've never had a cheating scumbag of a husband before."

She pushed herself up and walked to the oversized refrigerator. She had created a state-of-the-art kitchen for the inn, one in which she could expertly whip up breakfast for ten people every morning. But still the room retained its coziness, with whitewashed wood and mismatched antique stools. Olivia thought about all that was at risk here: Emily's marriage, her career as an innkeeper, her life in France.

"You're not talking," Olivia said.

Emily stared into the fridge. "I'm thinking," she murmured.

"About food or your marriage?"

"Same thing," Emily said. "I need them both to survive."

"You don't need Sébastien to survive."

Emily pushed the refrigerator door as if she were hoping for a resounding slam. But it whispered closed. She stood in front of the stainless-steel door, still searching for something.

"I don't know, O," Emily said, her voice weary. "I never thought I'd be in this situation. It's so French, it's such a cliché. But this is Sébastien, my Sébastien. It doesn't make sense to me."

She finally turned and looked at Olivia.

"What does he say?" Olivia asked gently.

Emily shook her head. "It's so stupid. I'm embarrassed to tell you."

"Me? You can tell me anything. I'm an expert on stupid. I spent twenty-two years married to a man who loved his business more than he loved me."

"Sébastien denies it."

"Come on."

"Really. He says she came on to him and he turned her down and so she created this drama to punish him."

"Do you believe him?" Olivia asked.

Again, Emily shook her head. "Not for a second."

"I'll tell you the truth," a voice said behind them.

They both spun around. Sébastien stood in the doorway, looking as if he had just woken up. His hair was tousled; his jeans hung low on his hips. He wasn't wearing a shirt and Olivia noticed that he was thicker than he used to be. Even handsome Sébastien showed signs of aging, she thought. Is that what sent him into another woman's arms? Fear of losing what he's got?

"Go away," Emily said without much conviction.

"I want to talk to you. Before the day begins and you won't come near me again."

"I'll leave," Olivia said.

"No," Emily said, and her hand shot out to grab Olivia's elbow. "Stay."

Olivia dropped back onto the stool.

Sébastien walked around to the other side of the center island and sat on one of the stools facing them.

"Get dressed," Emily commanded.

He looked around the room, grabbed an apron and tied it on over his bare chest. He looked like a hillbilly chef.

"I won't believe you, no matter what you say," Emily said. She pulled the notebook open and stared at it.

"I lost your trust, *chérie*," Sébastien said, his voice low and quiet. "I will win it back. I will do whatever I have to do to win you back."

Emily looked up and faced Sébastien. "You fucked that woman," she said.

Olivia flinched—the second time Emily had cursed in a day and a half. Olivia had always teased her about being so prudish about language but Emily had argued that she couldn't take a chance in her business—her clients would be horrified if she dropped an F bomb. In Olivia's theater world, "fuck" had become a meaningless hiccup.

Sébastien held Emily's gaze.

"Once," he said.

"Liar."

"It is true. *Une fois*."

"I don't believe you."

"I know. I will make you believe me. I will not lose you, *chérie*. I did a terrible thing. Once."

"I don't care how many times you fucked her."

"Once."

"Why does that matter? Do I get one free fuck now?"

"Can I tell you what happened?" Sébastien asked.

"I don't want to know," Emily said. Then she threw the notebook across the room. "Tell me what happened."

"We should talk about this alone," Sébastien said weakly.

"I don't want to be alone with you," Emily told him.

Olivia held her breath. She didn't want to be here, yet she wouldn't abandon her friend.

Sébastien placed his hands on the table in front of him and stared at them. They were paws really, the hands of a man who worked around the inn, painting, gardening, building. When he and Emily took over the inn, he gave away his New York suits and polished shoes. He was an even better-looking man in a work shirt and jeans.

"It was only once because I was sick about it."

"Bullshit."

"Em, let him tell the story."

"Shut up," Emily snapped.

They all sat quietly for a moment. The refrigerator hummed.

"It was about two months ago," Sébastien said, his voice low. "I met Luc at Le Fumoir."

"Luc," Emily said with disgust. Olivia had heard about Sébastien's old childhood friend. He was a version of Jake, Brody's friend. Luc didn't treat women with much respect.

"When I got there Luc already had a woman at the table. She was drunk and very affectionate with him—I thought maybe they knew each other. No—a few minutes later she was behaving the same way with me. And Luc got mad. I tried to leave but Luc beat me to it. I told the woman I would have one drink but then I was going home."

Olivia strained to follow his story. His English was good but his accent was so strong that the words were often unfamiliar. Om. Home.

"I walked her home when I was done," Sébastien said. "And when I got to her place I walked her in. I do not know what happened. I ended up having sex with her. And the minute it happened I hated every part of it."

"Bullshit," Emily spat.

Sébastien lowered his head. They waited for him. Finally he looked up.

"*Je t'aime,*" he said, his face crumbling. "I made a horrible mistake."

"Go away," Emily said.

"Why did she show up now?" Olivia asked him.

"She calls me. I will not talk to her. She threatened to tell you if I would not be her *amant.*" Her lover.

"You should have slept with her again," Emily said.

"I could not sleep with her again. I did not want to sleep with her ever again."

"*Mes amis,*" Olivia said. "I've got to go. I love you both but I hate this mess."

Emily nodded; her rage seemed gone. She looked tired and sad.

Olivia left the kitchen. She pulled the door closed behind her, then passed through the entryway and out the main door. She heard a gate opening below and watched as Brody came through, his clothes wet against his body, his hair slick with sweat, his smile broad across his face.

"My wife," he said.

"Not yet," she told him.

Later that morning, Olivia, Brody, and Fanny, Brody's mother, borrowed Ulysse and went for a walk in the hills of Cassis. Beyond their inn, the road narrowed to one lane. It meandered over green hills and through lush vineyards. The morning mist settled into the nooks and crannies of the valley, coating everything with a whisper of white. Occasionally they'd see a

stone farmhouse or an old ivy-covered villa; they'd hear barking dogs from every property. The sun inched over the rolling
hills to warm them as they followed Ulysse.

"Rent-a-Dog," Brody said, ruffling Ulysse's fur. "That'll
be my new business. Wherever you travel you should be able
to rent a good dog for companionship on a hike."

"And how do you manage this?" Olivia asked. "Where do
you get your dogs?"

"Shelters," Brody said. "Get those dogs out of their crates
and into the fresh air."

"Brilliant," Olivia said. "Do it."

Fanny eyed him. "Are you serious?"

"Yes. No. I'm not ready for retirement."

Olivia hated hearing him say it. And yet she knew it was
there in the silences at the end of each day, while she talked
about her work at the theater. Financially they might be able to
make do on her income and his savings, but the guy needed to
wake up in the morning eager to do something other than take
a walk.

"Go back to your work," Fanny said. "You were so good at
what you did."

"I can't, Mom," Brody told her. "No real demand for a
large-animal vet in San Francisco."

"There must be places outside of the city. Isn't there horse
country somewhere near there?"

"I talked to a vet hospital in Woodside and one in West
Marin. No one's looking to hire a guy in his fifties. They want
new blood to train. And someone who will grow old with
them."

"You've got lots of years before you grow old," Fanny argued.

"Tell the twenty-eight-year-old that. They look at me and see an old guy. An old guy who did things differently in the wilds of Wyoming."

"You did it just fine," Fanny said.

Olivia smiled. She liked Fanny and her gentle way with her son. No wonder he treated women so well.

But she hated the notion that he had given up his career because of her. That he was bored and restless because of her.

"Your father worked until he was seventy-five. It was good for him, gave him some meaning in his life. There were days—"

She stopped speaking abruptly; both Olivia and Brody looked at her.

She shook her head and waved her hand. "Never mind me," she said under her breath.

"You all right, Mom?" Brody asked.

"Fine. I'm fine." But the words seemed stuck in her throat.

"I don't understand him," Brody said. "I can't imagine what he's thinking."

"Oh, Lord," she moaned. "You didn't bring me out on this walk to save my marriage, did you?"

Olivia laughed. "Brody might make saving your marriage his full-time job."

"Nah," Brody said lightly. "My mother has every right to be miserable."

"Who said I was miserable?"

"I know you are," Brody said. He put his arm around his

mother and held her close to him as they walked. Fanny was a tall, solid woman; she fit well at Brody's side. Olivia could see the resemblance in their strong bodies, their confident posture, their choice of cowboy boots even though they were walking in the hills of France.

"It's not like I asked for this," Fanny said quietly.

Fanny had called Brody just a couple of months ago to tell him that his dad had walked out on her. After fifty-five years of marriage, he had given her only one reason: I want to be alone now.

Sam had become more and more hermit-like over the past year, spending hours in his cabin by the river, reading or thinking or whatever the hell he did down there. Olivia had asked Brody if he thought there was a chance that his dad had a girlfriend in the cabin. Hell no, Brody said. He's a damn recluse. And it's going to kill my mother.

Fanny had offered to move into a separate bedroom, to stop complaining about his retreats to the cabin, to travel with her widowed friend Lucy so that Sam would have more time alone. But no, he had made up his mind. He was moving out. She could keep the ranch as long as he could stay in the little cabin. He wouldn't bother her. She'd never see him. As if that's what she wanted.

Brody had flown out to Wyoming to spend a few days with Fanny. She was heartbroken but tough—she told him that ranch women didn't waste time with tears. Brody realized that he had only seen his mother cry a few times. At Grace's funeral. When their dog Creek was shot by a hunter. When her own mother died. Brody tried to visit his father at the cabin but each time he arrived he'd see a sign on the door: GONE FISH-

ING. His father knew Brody was in town. Apparently Sam's desire to be alone included cutting off his one son as well.

"Mom," Brody said now, as they crossed onto a path that wound its way up the hill between two properties. They followed Ulysse's wagging tail. "Do you think he's losing it? Alzheimer's or something?"

"No," Fanny said. "The man says he's clear as a bell. And that he's done with the human race."

Brody had always described Sam as a man who worked too much. Brody's childhood was a happy one because he loved the ranch, his horses, his dogs. His mom created the kind of house that friends wanted to come to and that's where they'd hang out, getting stoned in the barn, making out with girlfriends in the hayloft. Sam, a doctor, was always somewhere else—at the clinic doing rounds, driving across the county for house calls, delivering babies in the middle of the night. When Sam stopped practicing medicine Brody thought that his parents would travel, explore, perhaps even buy a small apartment in San Francisco.

"So why this change?" Brody said. "Why would he leave you?"

"I wanted more of him," Fanny said softly. "I was getting lonely in my old age."

Olivia slipped her arm through Fanny's. There was something so soothing about this woman's honesty. Olivia had lost her own mom a few years earlier. She missed her parents with a physical ache, one that would stab at her in the middle of the night or at some odd point in her day when she'd think: I'll call and tell Mom. Still, after three years. Having Fanny in her life might ease that loss.

They walked in silence for a while. Fanny had no trouble with the steep path. She was remarkably fit for seventy-six—she still rode her horse for an hour or so every day. She did many of her own chores on the ranch, though now Ed, her ranch hand, helped her with the harder ones.

"Dad should have come to my wedding," Brody said, shaking his head.

Brody had been furious with Sam for refusing to come. When Brody had finally reached Sam by phone, his dad said he couldn't make it, he was too old, he didn't travel anymore. None of that was true. "Do it for me," Brody had countered. But Sam had simply said, "Can't make it, son," and that was the end of that.

"Bastard," Fanny said.

"I'll come out again," Brody said. "I'll make him talk to me this time."

"It won't work," Fanny said. "You know that, Brody."

Brody stopped walking, mid-trail, pulled out his cellphone and tapped on a number.

"What are you doing?" Fanny asked, reaching for the phone. Brody turned away.

"It's the middle of the night in Wyoming," Olivia argued.

Brody ignored them, listening while the phone rang. He stepped away when Sam answered and both women watched him.

"It's me. Brody."

He listened for a moment.

"No. No emergency. I have to catch you sleeping so you'll accidentally pick up the phone."

Fanny shook her head and sat down on a rock. Olivia joined her.

"I'm in France, Dad," Brody said. "It's my wedding weekend."

His voice was dark. Olivia could feel Fanny's body stiffen beside her.

"You're pissing off a lot of people who care about you," Brody said.

He walked away and then he, too, sat on a rock, far from the women. They could no longer hear his conversation.

Ulysse poked his nose into Olivia's leg. "Soon, sweet dog," she said.

Brody ended the call and put the cellphone back in his pocket. He walked over to Fanny and sat by her side, his arm around her.

"Dad's stubborn as hell." His voice broke.

"I know that, Brody," Fanny said. She sat erect and proud on the rock.

"He's done with people, he says." Brody looked out toward a grove of olive trees. "With all of us."

"It's got nothing to do with you," Fanny said.

Brody nodded. "It's my wedding weekend and he couldn't give a damn."

Olivia felt a rush of emotion for Brody. And then she thought of both of them—wife and son, losing Sam in their lives. You open yourself up to love and you face the hell of loss.

"We'll get along without him," Fanny announced, pushing herself up from the rock.

They started walking again and found themselves on the top of a ridge with a view of the harbor of Cassis and the Mediterranean beyond. The red cliffs shimmered against the teal blue sea. A hawk circled above them.

"I'll come out and visit soon," Brody told his mother. Olivia could hear the pain in his voice.

Fanny nodded, walking with her head down. As if Ulysse could sense her distress, he moved to her side. Fanny's hand brushed his fur as they walked.

"Thanks, Ulysse," Brody said. "You're a damn good Rent-a-Dog. You're my inspiration."

"No," Fanny said, shaking her head. "There are so many other things you can do with your life."

"I'm not finding them," Brody said, and his voice sounded tight in his throat.

"But you're happy in San Francisco?" Fanny asked, and Olivia felt a flash of anger. It's not my fault, she wanted to say. He chose to come live with me.

"Yes," Brody said, reaching for Olivia's hand. But for the first time Olivia thought: *Is* he happy? Has he given up too much? What if he doesn't find a job?

Her cellphone chirped in her pocket.

"Damn," she muttered, pulling it out. A text message from Nell.

He's gone. He fucking left. Mom, come back.

Olivia showed the message to Brody.

"Go," he said. "We'll catch up with you."

"You sure?" she asked.

"My mom and I could use a little time up here," Brody said with a nod.

Olivia felt a twinge of abandonment—no, she was the one abandoning him. How do we come together? Olivia thought. My girls. His parents. My life in San Francisco. His life in Wyoming.

Her cellphone chirped again.

"Daughter crisis," Olivia told Fanny. "Tell me something. When do you stop being a mother?"

"Never," Fanny said. "Thank God."

Olivia kissed them both and then took off, running down the trail and back to the inn.

Chapter Eight

Nell sat in the middle of the bed, crying. She had woken late, the sun already flooding the room, and when she had reached for Gavin, she knew in an instant he was gone.

She had said too much. She had asked too much.

She heard a knock on the door.

"Who is it?" she called, her voice wobbly.

"It's me," her mother said.

Nell got up, opened the door and let her mom in. She fell into her arms.

"What happened?" Olivia asked.

Nell sat back on the edge of the bed, wiping her face with her sleeve. She wore the black button-down shirt that Gavin had worn to dinner last night. She had slept in it at some point during the night. It was the only thing of his left in the room.

"I'm such a dope," Nell said, and she began to cry again.

Olivia sat beside her and moved her hand in slow circles on her back.

"Shhhh," she murmured.

"Why do I do this?" Nell asked. "I meet a guy and I decide that he's the one and I figure that out in like twenty-four hours and then a second later he's gone?"

"You open yourself up too easily," Olivia said quietly. "That's always been true."

"And what am I supposed to do? Steel myself? Play by someone's rules that say you can't sleep with a guy until the third date."

"Well, that would be a place to start."

"Did you sleep with Brody the night you met him?"

"I'm not answering that."

"You don't have to."

She caught her mother's easy smile. Both women lay back on the bed, staring at the ceiling above them.

"You took a chance, sweetheart," Olivia said. "It didn't work out. It's not the end of the world."

Nell took her mother's hand.

"He didn't even leave a note," Nell said.

Chaney hadn't left a note. She had searched for one everywhere—he owed her a note! How could he kill himself without telling her why? She'd spent long nights imagining that note. He could have told her that he was miserable and bipolar and he could have told her that he loved her and always would and she was the best part of his life and he was so so sorry to do this to her.

That note didn't exist. Instead, his silence accused her. She should have known. She should have saved him.

"He's not worth all these tears," Olivia said.

Nell was confused for a moment and then realized they were talking about Gavin.

"I don't know," Nell said. "He was pretty damn sexy."

"And sexy takes off in the morning."

"So I should look for boring? Unappealing? Ugly as hell? Those are the guys who stay?"

"No," Olivia said.

"I don't want anyone to know," Nell told her.

"What do you mean?"

"I'm embarrassed. Everyone thinks I'm such a flake anyway. And then my guy ditches me. He can't even wait for the wedding."

"I don't want any assholes at my wedding," Olivia said.

Nell smiled. "You're right."

The sound of laughter drifted through the open window. Then Jake called out, "Where are all the pretty French girls?" and someone hooted.

"*Les filles! Les filles!*" Jake yelled.

"We can tell everyone he had a family emergency," Olivia said.

Nell laughed. "I don't even know if the guy has a family!"

"That's the emergency," Olivia said. "He went off in search of one."

Nell squeezed her hand. "Thanks, Mom."

"I didn't like him anyway," Olivia said.

"Neither did I," Nell lied.

She thought of Chaney again. Alone. In the bed she shared with him. She had gone for a haircut. She couldn't wait to show him her pixie cut. She raced home on her bike and walked into the apartment shouting, "Your sexy lover is home!" She knew right away that something was wrong, even before she walked into the bedroom.

"Let's go eat breakfast," Olivia said, standing.

Nell shook her head. "Carly's going to lord this one over me."

"You girls aren't teenagers anymore."

"Like OMG, really?" Nell said, smiling. "We just act like teenagers."

"It's time to try something else," Olivia said.

"Go on down," Nell said. "I'll take a shower and put on some makeup so I don't scare the guests. I'll be down soon."

Olivia leaned over and kissed the top of Nell's head. Then she left the room.

Nell stood and walked to the window. She could see someone doing laps in the pool. Jake, the only happy guy at the inn because he was devoted to staying single. But I want love, Nell thought. I want Chaney back.

Chapter Nine

Carly walked along the narrow winding road that led from the inn to the harbor. She wanted some exercise; she wanted to buy croissants at a pâtisserie in town and bring them back for everyone. She wanted a better day.

Her night had been ragged—too many nightmares, most of them slipping through her fingers the moment she awoke. Someone was holding her underwater. She and Wes were yelling to each other across a great expanse of snow but no words escaped their lips.

She tried to shake the images from her mind. Clean country air, warm sun, the smell of rosemary. Next time she'd bring sleeping pills when she traveled.

She knew that she was drifting away from Wes. The snowy

expanse between them. The unheard shouts. Perhaps she
needed less comfort in a relationship. He was a brilliant friend
and boss, someone she should meet for drinks and conversation about work. Not a guy to live with, not a guy to love. Next
time she'd fall for an artist, a rock star, a handyman. Someone
who touched her soul instead of her mind. Frankly, she was a
little tired of her mind these days.

Why did she think that her relationship with Wes had anything to do with love? She remembered when Nell asked her if
she was sleeping with her boss to further her career. That's
ridiculous, she countered. He might be sleeping with me to
keep me from stealing it all away from him. But the issue
wasn't sleeping together. It was the pretense of love. Besides,
the sex was merely competent. She wanted crazy sex, the kind
of sex that had Nell and her guy banging against the wall all
hours of the night.

My God, Carly thought. I've never envied my sister before. I must be coming undone.

She walked fast, trying to break a sweat. She'd feel better if
she could get her endorphins going. Right now it felt as if she
were slogging through air made thick with last night's dreams.

A car honked lightly and she moved over to the side of the
road. There's plenty of room, she thought. Just pass me already.

But the car inched forward and then stopped. The driver
tapped on the horn again.

"Yo. Carly!"

She saw Nell's guy, leaning over the passenger seat to reach
for the door.

"Get in!"

She shook her head. "I'm good," she said. "I need the exercise."

"Get in," he said again. "We'll exercise later."

Is he flirting with me? Of course he is—the guy flirts with everyone. She had caught him last night with his eyes on her across the dinner table. And now one side of his mouth lifted in a mischievous grin.

Why the hell didn't *she* ever have a one-night stand? Might be good for her to live inside her body instead of her mind. But this was Nell's date, Nell's one-night stand. Was the night over and he was moving on?

"Quick—a car is coming," he said, and he pushed open the passenger door.

She slid into the seat and looked behind her. No car was coming.

He took off, speeding down the country road.

"Where are you headed so early?" she asked.

"I wanted to explore the area," he said. "And look what I found. A sister."

He was too damn pleased with himself. Where were his black glasses? He looked younger without them. Or older? He drove the car with one hand on the wheel, one arm on the window frame, his hand tapping on the roof as if he could hear a song in the silence. He wore a black T-shirt with the short sleeves pushed up, biceps bulging. Who is this guy?

"I'm just headed to town," she told him. "You can drop me off when you get close to the harbor."

"Maybe we'll take a drive together," he said.

"Why would we do that?" she asked. She felt like someone

other than herself. A woman who might hop into a guy's car and take off. Not knowing where they might go.

"Scared of me?"

He reached out his hand and she thought he was going to touch her leg. She inched over in her seat, closer to the door. But he tapped on the radio and the sound of a woman singing plaintively of *amour* burst forth.

She shook her head. "Not at all," she said. "I know my sister likes you. I'm staying away." Though she was thinking about a long drive along the coast, the open windows, the briny smell of the sea, *l'amour*.

"You won't," he said.

"I won't what?"

"Stay away."

She started to laugh and then stopped. She looked at him again. Was he dangerous? He's just a boy, she thought. A sexy boy, his eyes on her legs.

He turned the knob and the music got louder, too loud.

Carly felt herself stiffen. Ahead she saw a sign: CENTRE VILLE. He sped toward the intersection and then turned left, away from the center of town and the harbor and the pâtisserie.

"Where are we going?" she asked. She pushed fear away.

"Where would you like to go?" he asked, his eyes on the road ahead.

She thought of a conversation with Wes only a week ago. "If you want to run this business one day you have to stop analyzing every little decision," he told her. "Don't think so much. Act."

Gavin turned the music louder until it filled all the space of the car.

"Somewhere," she said. "Anywhere."

She reached into her purse, her fingers trembling, and turned off her cellphone.

And then he said something, his words lost in the noise, a dreamy smile on his face. An adventure, she thought. That's what he said.

"Yes," she told him.

Part Two

Chapter Ten

Olivia tried Carly's cellphone for the third time and again the call went immediately to voice mail. She threw her phone on the bed.

Ulysse gazed at her quizzically. She had let him follow her into the room earlier and now he lay in the middle of the rug, watching her every move.

"Carly never goes anywhere without her phone," she told him.

He raised one eyebrow and then the other.

Olivia sat on the floor beside the dog, resting her hand on his head.

When Carly was in high school she slept with her phone on her pillow. Some girls had teddy bears; her daughter cuddled with the Internet. She was never much of a child, even at four

or five. When Olivia would meet other moms in Dolores Park
the kids would chase each other, climb trees, invent games. Big
sister Nell was one of the gang, often getting lost in the park if
Olivia didn't pay close enough attention. But Carly would sit
by Olivia's side, observing the adult world, as if preparing for
her own role in it.

No, she wasn't preparing to be a mom. She was preparing
to run the world.

Stop worrying about her, Brody said last month. She's
happy the way she is. Not everyone's cut from the same mold.
But Olivia did worry. She didn't think Carly knew how to
have fun. It didn't matter how smart she was or how ambitious,
the girl needed to learn how to balance her life in some way.
Before she turned into her father.

The door opened and Olivia leapt to her feet as if caught
doing something wrong. And then she remembered: She was
supposed to be getting dressed for kayaking. Everyone was
waiting for her. And now Brody was here to drag her out into
the world.

"She's nowhere," Olivia said. "She's not in her room.
She's not answering her phone."

"Carly?" Brody asked.

"No one has seen her since last night."

He walked toward her and took her in his arms.

"I'm not going without her," Olivia said into his shoulder.

He pulled back and looked at her. "What?"

"Kayaking. Calanquing. Whatever it is."

"Kayaking in the calanques. You have to come."

"I'll wait until Carly shows up. Ulysse and I are going to
stay right here."

Again Brody tried to press her to him. This time she wiggled away.

"I'm serious," she said, folding her arms across her chest.

"I see that."

"Besides, my arms are too weak for kayaking."

"That's why we're partners. I'll do all the work."

Olivia dropped onto the bed. Ulysse lifted himself off the floor and nuzzled his head onto her lap. "You keep distracting me by being so damn nice," she said.

"I'll try to stop that." Brody kissed the top of her head.

"I'll walk downstairs with you," Olivia said. "I'll make some excuse and you'll all go off and have a grand time and I'll be sitting here with Carly, drinking champagne, when you get back. Ulysse will be at my side, breathing dog breath in my face."

"You sure?"

"Very. Carly knew what time we were leaving. She didn't even show up for breakfast. That girl has never skipped breakfast in her life."

"I'm sure she walked into town," Brody said. "She's probably sitting in a café right now, feasting on a decadent pastry. She just needed a little time by herself."

"You're wrong. I know my daughter."

Brody nodded. He was quiet for a moment and Olivia imagined his thoughts: She needs to let her daughters go. She needs to let them be adults in the world. Or were those her own thoughts? If Carly were home in Palo Alto, Olivia would have no idea where she was and she wouldn't have any reason to worry. Why turn into an overprotective mom just because her daughters were spending the weekend with her?

Her phone, sitting in the middle of the bed, rang loudly, setting off a round of barking by Ulysse. Olivia threw herself on the bed, grabbing the phone.

"Carly?"

"Mom. Sorry, I had the phone turned off."

"Where are you?"

"In town. Went for a walk."

Olivia felt her body ease, as if someone released the knot inside of her.

"We're leaving for the kayak trip. Should we pick you up?"

"I need some time alone," Carly said. "Do you mind?"

"You're going to miss the kayaking trip?" Olivia glanced at Brody who was watching her. He wants her there, she thought. He organized this trip and he's trying to win Carly over. She can't bail.

"I'm going for a walk by the sea," Carly said. "Work has been hell the last two weeks. We're gearing up for an international launch and I've been dealing with hundreds of interviews for new country managers. I just need a little time on my own."

"Carly, we have two days here together. Take time alone after the wedding. Brody planned this—"

"I'll see you later in the day," Carly said. "I gotta go. Love you." She clicked off, ending the call.

"What the hell?" Olivia said.

"She okay?" Brody asked.

Olivia nodded. "The girl needs a break," she said. "I guess I can't argue with that."

Brody offered a hand and pulled her up. Standing next to him, she smelled pine forest and ocean air. She placed her hand on his chest, as if reaching for the smell. She wanted to unbutton his shirt and press her face into the heat of his skin.

Be a bride, not a mom.

"I'll come calanquing," Olivia said.

Ulysse moved to her side as if she had given the right command.

"Good," Brody said, smiling. "That's not a word but let's do it."

"Promise you'll be my partner. I don't want anyone else to know about my weak arms."

"I'm your partner," Brody said.

"You're my partner," Olivia said, testing the words in her mouth.

Olivia walked out of the inn, Ulysse at her heels, and saw the group gathered in the garden. Brody, Nell, Jake, Fanny, Sébastien.

"Where's Emily?" she called.

"At the *marché*," Sébastien said. Ulysse immediately bounded off to sit at Sébastien's side. "She has too much to do. She will meet us back here for a late lunch."

Olivia had too much to do. She had to console her best friend, help her prepare lunch, swim a few hundred laps in the pool until her mind cleared and her heart settled. But she saw Nell's sad face and Brody's hopeful look and so she clapped her hands and called out, "What are you all waiting for?"

She headed down the hill toward the parking lot and heard the murmurs and mumbling from the group as they fell in behind her.

"We'll take our car and Sébastien's," Brody said while they walked. "Fanny, you'll come with us. Jake and Nell ride with Sébastien."

"I've only got the motorcycle," Sébastien said. "Emily's got our car."

"Nell," Brody said. "Do you mind driving?"

"I didn't bring my keys," Nell said. "Hang on—I'll run back."

"I've got mine," Jake said. "I can drive."

They turned into the parking lot and headed toward the two cars.

"My car is gone!" Nell shouted. She stood in front of an empty parking spot.

"Gavin?" Olivia asked.

Nell's chin quivered. "He fucking stole my rental car!"

Olivia walked over and put her arm around her. "Are you sure?"

"Where else is it? He disappeared and the damn car disappeared."

Olivia felt a gut punch of fury. She knew Gavin was bad but hadn't thought that he was criminal bad. She pulled away from her daughter. How could Nell have been such an idiot?

"Great date," Olivia said, the words out of her mouth before she could stop herself.

"God damn you," Nell growled. She turned and stormed off, heading up the hill toward the inn.

"Come back," Olivia called, her voice shaky. "Nell. It's just a car. Your insurance will cover it. No one got hurt."

She looked at Brody, who stepped away from the group. The others pretended to ignore the family drama—they gathered around each other, kicking stones, gazing up at the cypress trees, checking their cellphones.

"We should call the police," Brody said to her quietly.

The police. Nell and her damn troublemaking life.

"I'll go get her," Olivia said. "Ask Sébastien to call the police."

"And then we go calanquing?" Brody asked.

"It's not a word," Olivia said as she started up the hill.

"You're coming back?" he called after her.

"Of course I'm coming back," she said. "How could you possibly manage a kayak without me?"

She found Nell by the pool, sitting on the edge, her bare feet dangling in the water. Olivia felt as if all of the drama of Nell's childhood unfolded this way: The girl would fight, then flee. Twenty-eight years old and nothing had changed.

Olivia slipped off her flip-flops and sat beside her. "I'm sorry," she said.

Nell fluttered her feet in the water.

"I shouldn't have said that," Olivia said.

"I'm not mad at you," Nell said, her feet suddenly still. "I'm mad at myself."

"So you won't pick up guys on airplanes anymore," Olivia said. "Lesson learned. Now we go kayaking and enjoy a pretty glorious day."

For the first time, Olivia noticed the day: The sky, clear of clouds, was a brilliant shade of blue. Around them the field of wildflowers rustled in the breeze. The sun had already baked the sandstone patio and Olivia guessed that the day would be very warm.

"Really?" Nell said.

"What?"

"That's it? I fucked up, he stole my car, and we move on?"

"Yes," Olivia said, her voice strong. "It doesn't do any of us any good to be miserable about this. It's over. He's over. Now let's celebrate my wedding weekend."

Nell slid into the pool. She was wearing yoga shorts and a tank top. She pulled off the tank top and threw it onto the deck of the pool. She kept her back—now clothed in a bikini top—to her mother.

Olivia waited. She thought about Brody, waiting for her. All the others, waiting for her. Come on, Nell. I don't have time for this.

Nell spun around as if she could hear her mother's thoughts. "That's what I don't get," she said, her voice sharp.

"What?" Olivia asked, suddenly weary.

"How you do that. Move on. Chaney dies and you think I should be over it already."

"I never said that."

"You said it the day you left L.A. Get over it, Nell. Move on. Move on. It's your fucking mantra."

"It's not my mantra. I don't have a fucking mantra." Olivia felt anger rising from somewhere deep inside her. Don't let her do this to you, she thought.

"You have some superpower that the rest of us mere mortals are lacking," Nell spat from the center of the pool. "You fail as an actress, you become head of the damn theater company. You lose the lease on your theater, you get offered space in fancier digs at the same cheap rate. You divorce my dad, you find a hotter guy. You're the queen of moving on and I can't get out of bed most days. I can't stop thinking about what I did wrong and what I might have said to change things. I see Chaney lying in our bed every time I close my eyes. Did you know that he was naked? Why? Why didn't I throw away my old sleeping pills? Why didn't he tell me how much he wanted that goddamn role? Why didn't he tell me he was bipolar? Six months later and I can't fucking move on."

Olivia slid into the pool. Her long beach tunic wrapped around her. She tried walking toward Nell but the cloth tangled between her legs. She dropped underwater and pulled the dress over her head. It floated like a ghost beside her.

In her bathing suit Olivia felt lighter and freer. She walked toward Nell.

"Don't touch me," Nell said.

"I can't stand your pain," Olivia said.

"Don't," Nell said. "Don't tell me what I should do and how I should be."

Olivia felt clearer than she had all weekend. "When I tell you to move on, it's because I can't stand how much you hurt and I want it to go away. I'm your mother. I adore you." She stopped walking and faced her daughter. "I'm wrong. I can't make it go away."

She saw tears sliding down Nell's face.

"I can listen to you," Olivia said. "That's what I can do."

She reached out and took Nell into her arms.

"My girl," Olivia said, her head pressed against Nell's. "My sad, wonderful girl."

The dreadlocked young man at the kayak center looked stoned and bored. He tossed life vests into the boats as if they were a nuisance, something only tourists would wear. Olivia grabbed hers, now wet and cold from the dirty water on the bottom of the boat, and slipped her arms through it. Suddenly the dude was interested. He stepped forward and strapped the vest across her chest, breathing cannabis breath on her face.

He mumbled something in rapid-fire French. Olivia stepped away. "I don't speak French," she said, though she usually managed well enough. But this guy was rattling on way too quickly. Besides, she was angry at all the young men who could cause her daughter pain.

"And the paddles?" she asked in English. "Where are they?"

He had moved on to help Nell with her vest and Olivia felt the urge to punch him. But Nell stepped away and adjusted her own straps. Good for her, Olivia thought.

Brody emerged from a cabin with an armful of paddles. He began distributing them to everyone.

"Jake, you're with Nell," he said and immediately Olivia thought: No, not Jake. But Nell happily climbed into the kayak. At least she's smiling, Olivia told herself.

"Sébastien, my mother will do all the work, so you have nothing to worry about," Brody said.

"Alors," Sébastien said. "Fanny, you are in the rear."

"I am not," Fanny said.

Olivia saw Fanny's frailty for the first time. She looked old in her bathing suit, her skin sagging, her body trembling. She imagined what Fanny might be thinking: Sam's my partner. I need Sam.

"Bon," Sébastien said. "I'll have to manage in the back."

He climbed in, his athletic body at ease in the kayak.

"And you, my love," Brody said, turning toward Olivia, "may sit here."

He gestured to the bow of the kayak beside him. Olivia blew him a kiss and climbed into her seat.

"Follow me, gang," Brody called. "We're going to head west and turn in at the fourth calanque. We'll explore there and then head back, turning in at the third and the first. Apparently the best swimming is in the one called d'En-vau. But we'll see how it goes. If anyone's too tired—and I know that would be Jake, poor guy—just let me know and we'll change our plans."

"We're leaving you in the dust," Jake said.

He hopped into the kayak and pushed off. Nell grabbed the sides of the boat and then settled in, already laughing. She needs a good time, Olivia thought.

Jake pulled off his T-shirt and began paddling. Olivia noticed that even though he was shorter than Brody, his shoulders were broader, his muscles more defined. He was a sun-scorched guy with wheat-blond hair. Not my type, Olivia thought. Whatever that meant. In fact, for a year now, she had only had one type: Brody. That was a surprise to her after so many years of sexual curiosity. Even before her marriage ended, seven years ago, she started noticing all the good-looking men who inhabited her world. There were actors, directors, patrons, theatergoers. There were doctors and dentists and lawyers. The world was full of hot guys. She was so starved for sexual attention that she turned on the male world with laser eyes. You're out there and I want you.

Oddly, once she was divorced, she didn't go wild. She dated

a few men and found them attractive but self-absorbed. They were too damn cocky. They were hung up on young women. They were insecure. Desire turned out to be much more fun than the real deal. Until she met Brody.

And now she forgot about all the other hot guys out there. Watching Jake reminded her how foreign it was for her to admire another man's body or to think about kissing that guy. No, she didn't want to kiss Jake. She wanted to warn her daughter: Stay away.

She fell into an easy paddling rhythm, stroking on the left, then on the right. Brody did whatever he needed to do behind her to direct them and propel them forward at a surprisingly fast pace. They breezed by Jake and Nell's kayak, ignoring their trash talk. And in moments they were out in the open sea, the dramatic limestone cliffs rising up on their right.

Olivia felt a breeze on her arms and she noticed whitecaps for the first time. Emily had told her about the storms in the south of France, the mistrals. These winds keep the clouds away. When the wind stops, the clouds gather and a storm batters the coast. Not on my wedding day, she thought.

"Hang on," Brody called to her. "Let's give Sébastien and my mother a chance to catch up."

Olivia drew her paddle out of the water and laid it across the front of the kayak. Brody moved their boat around so they could watch the others paddle toward them.

"I love this," Olivia said.

"So that means you'll trust me from here on in?"

"Not a chance," she told him.

"The color of the sea keeps changing with the light," Brody said. "I've never seen so many shades of blue."

"No wonder so many artists lived in the south of France," Olivia said. "There's something about the light that makes the world look brand new."

"And the sea air," he said. "I was landlocked for too many years."

"Maybe it's love that's distorting our vision," Olivia said, looking back at him.

"Damn right." Brody beamed at her.

During the six years that she was single she did just fine in the world, running her business, meeting friends for dinner or a movie, taking a theater trip to London every year by herself. She wasn't lonely, or at least she kept busy enough not to notice it very often. But after she met Brody, she felt the world shift somehow. She talked to him about everything, as if all of it—her daughters, her theater, her fears and passions— belonged to both of them. Now she wondered if loneliness had hidden somewhere for all those years, just out of sight.

Nell and Jake pulled up in their kayak. Nell's face was flushed and her eyes shone.

"Man, is it gorgeous out here!" she said.

"And we haven't even entered the calanques yet," Brody told her.

"You are fools!" Sébastien called, edging closer with Fanny in the last kayak. He was working hard to make his way toward them. "You are doing this all wrong. You should take your time and look around. This is not a race. This is a way of living on the water."

But he was smiling as Nell splashed him with her paddle. He splashed her back, soaking her with the chilly seawater, when suddenly a speedboat raced behind them, sending up an enormous wake. Olivia saw her paddle slipping from the boat and lunged for it just in time, then gripped the sides of the kayak, trying to regain her balance. She heard shouts from Brody, and then suddenly their kayak lunged left and right again.

She heard a scream and turned back. With a new wave, Sébastien and Fanny's kayak capsized, toppling them both into the water.

Brody dove from behind her into the sea.

Olivia looked around the boat, fear surging through her veins and turning her suddenly cold.

And then she saw Fanny's head bobbing in the water. Sébastien was hanging on to the bottom of their upturned kayak. Was Fanny wearing her life vest? Could she swim?

"Reach my hand!" Sébastien shouted to Fanny.

"I can't—" she yelled and then her head went under.

Brody appeared close to the spot where she went down.

"To your right!" Olivia screamed. "She's right there!"

Brody dove down and then Jake dove into the water as well. Nell shouted as her own kayak almost toppled.

Olivia was about to dive in when Brody emerged, his mother in his arms. She was coughing and pushing against him.

"Leave me alone!" Fanny shouted.

Brody pulled her over toward Sébastien and the now up-right kayak, holding one arm across her chest.

"I'm fine, goddamn it!" Fanny yelled. "I know how to swim, for Christ's sake."

Nell started laughing. "Look at the three of you," she called. "Three heroes in search of a damsel in distress."

"Well, I'm no damsel," Fanny said. "Brody, let me go right now or I'm going to smack you."

Brody released her. She put her arms on the side of the kayak and rested for a moment.

"Need a hand?" Brody asked sheepishly.

"Not on your life," Fanny said. She pulled herself up and into the boat. Nell and Olivia cheered wildly.

"My God," Nell said. "There is way too much testosterone around here."

Brody hauled himself up into the kayak with his mother.

He looked back, avoiding Olivia's eyes. "We're switching teams," he said.

And then suddenly her kayak lurched and Jake climbed into the back.

"Is this musical chairs?" Olivia asked, unsure about her new partner.

"Or spin the bottle," Jake said with a grin.

"Spare me," Olivia groaned.

Sébastien climbed into the kayak with Nell and they were off again, following Brody and Fanny as they headed west.

"Brody's worried about his mother," Olivia said, her jaw set as she began to paddle again.

"He's a good son," Jake said. "Always has been."

Olivia turned back, surprised. Jake was Brody's oldest childhood friend. Of course he knew Brody's relationship with his mom.

"I would hate to fall in love with a man who hated his mom," Olivia said. "Bad sign, I think."

"Good thing you didn't fall in love with me," Jake told her.

"I haven't seen my mother in six years. The woman's a holy terror. I need to stay away to stay sane."

Olivia looked back at him.

"Keep paddling," he called.

She spun around and fell back into a rhythm, stroking left, then right. She imagined Jake behind her, watching. It made her uneasy. Something about him unnerved her. They had met once before, when she visited Brody in Wyoming. The three of them went to a small-town music concert, set up on an empty lot by the river. One band played what they called western blues and another band played roots rock. Olivia loved the crowd—families, western hipsters, old hippies, and cowboys. Jake spent all his time on the dance floor, grinding with the prettiest girls.

Jake made Olivia feel old. With most people she was the bohemian, the theater person, the Californian freethinker. But she found herself judging Jake. Why didn't he grow up? Why didn't he settle down?

Why was he solid, reliable Brody's best friend? Why was he going to perform their wedding ceremony tomorrow?

When they told him they were getting married he had sent Brody an email. *No fucking way, Brody. Do I have to come out there and save you? Live a little. Live a lot. Why turn into a married man again?*

"Why do you like this guy?" Olivia had asked Brody.

"We have a long history together," Brody had told her. Which told her nothing.

"Just give him a chance," he had insisted. "Do it for me."

But did she have to spend the morning kayaking with him?

Of course Jake hated his mother. He probably hated all women.

"Do you have women friends?" she asked Jake now.

"I was very close with Grace," he told her.

Olivia felt it like a slap across her face.

"Tell me about her," she said. Her paddle smacked against the water. She had lost her rhythm. She could feel Jake behind her, trying to correct the boat's direction.

"She was very different from you," he said.

"How so?"

"In about a million different ways," Jake told her.

And then he fell silent, leaving her to fill in the blanks.

Olivia tried to settle herself by falling into a comfortable rhythm with the paddle: stroke, lift, twist; stroke, lift, twist. Sure enough, her arms were growing tired. But she wouldn't admit that to Jake; she powered on.

Grace probably had superwoman arms, she thought.

As they passed the first opening in the cliffs she finally could see what a calanque was all about. A long finger of water stretched inland, bordered by immense limestone cliffs. The iridescent blue water shimmered against the dazzling white rock.

"Take a look!" she called to Jake.

"Want to blow off the group and go explore?" he yelled back.

She felt a flash of anger. Brody's the leader, not you. Brody's my partner, not you.

"No," she said. "We're supposed to go in backwards order. We'll see this one last."

"Aha. So you'll be a dutiful wife?"

She spun around and glared at him. He was smiling devilishly.

She turned away. "Brody and I will be good for each other," she said. "I'm sure of that."

"How can you be sure?" he asked. "What if another guy catches your eye?"

"I don't think so, Jake."

"You're a beautiful woman," he said. "I'm sure there are lots of men who hit on you."

She shook her head. He was testing her. He wanted to know if he could warn his buddy against her. She wouldn't play his game.

Her arms pushed the paddle through the water with a surge of new energy. I can't compete with Saint Grace. I'm not her. I'm me.

Chapter Eleven

Nell and Sébastien were the last to pull up to the beach at the end of the calanque. Nell had finally figured out how to paddle, using Sébastien's advice. "You told me you practice yoga," he had said when he saw her slapping the water with each stroke. "Try zen kayaking."

"What the hell is that?" Nell asked, wet from the constant splashing of her paddle, annoyed that she had lost Jake as a partner. He was sexy and distracting. She needed a major distraction.

"Breathe through each stroke. Just like yoga. Make your breath long and steady. Same with the stroke."

Not a chance, she thought. But she started to match her breath with each stroke. Soon, the strokes lengthened and her heart eased. The kayak glided through the water.

"It worked!" she called back to him.

"*Je sais,*" he told her.

"Zen kayaking," she said, pleased.

So they zen kayaked to shore and finally abandoned the boat, pulled it up high on the beach, and walked to join the others.

Nell stayed back for a moment, watching the group, their feet in the water, staring out to sea. She was the kid among them, though at twenty-eight she should stop thinking of herself as a kid. But they seemed like a different species to her—they had jobs and homes and history. She had nothing. She felt unformed, as if she were still hoping to wake up one morning and recognize herself in the mirror. There I am. Nell, an adult in the world. This is what I do; this is where I'm headed.

Her mother and Jake stood to one side, in the middle of some kind of argument. Olivia was always over-animated when she was angry. Now she gestured madly with her hands, as if speaking sign language. And her body emanated excess energy. Nell could see that Jake was smiling, either amused by Olivia's outburst or doing his best not to let her get under his skin. Nell liked the wicked smile.

Sébastien offered Fanny a towel that Brody then wrapped around her shoulders. Nell stepped up to them and breathed in the sea air. I belong here, too, she told herself.

The mountains that hugged this spit of water were sheer and luminous. The sea lapped up against the rock, blue and white so startlingly bright that Nell squinted in the glare of so much color.

She relaxed her shoulders and let her arms drop. They were

weary from paddling. She let a slow breath run through her, calming her.

Then Gavin flitted through her mind like a gnat, disturbing her peace. She imagined him driving her lousy rental car, picking up a hitchhiker, a pretty young French girl with a short skirt. She imagined his eyes on her thighs.

No. She swatted the gnat away.

"Who wants to swim?" she called out.

The group startled as if all of them had been caught in a trance.

"Race you to the rock!" Brody shouted, his body catapulting forward so that in three long strides he could dive into the water.

Nell saw a low flat rock that protruded from one side of the inlet. It was halfway down the finger of water, a long swim from the beach.

"You're on!" Nell shouted, though Brody could no longer hear her.

She ran until the water was deep enough and then dove into all that blue.

She swam quickly, her tired arms pushing her forward. Her muscles trembled with the effort. Zen swimming, she thought. She found a rhythm to her stroke, slow and steady, and soon her arms started to float overhead, one and then the other, propelling her forward. Her head was filled with the sound of the sea.

She imagined Chaney swimming at her side. They matched their strokes, their stride, their smiles. We'll make love on that rock, she thought. Black rock, blue sea, white cliffs. And your long body next to mine. When we make love you'll come home to me.

She swallowed water, too much water. She coughed and sputtered and blinked the salty water from her eyes.

"You okay?" she heard.

Brody bobbed by her side.

"You were underwater too long," he said.

"I'm fine," she said quickly. But she wasn't fine. She had lost Chaney and Gavin and now she was gasping for air in the calm Mediterranean Sea.

"We're almost at the rock," Brody said. "Catch your breath."

"Not in the middle of a race," Nell insisted and pushed herself forward one more time.

Brody swam behind her, probably so that he'd scoop her up if she sank underwater. There was something so heroic about him, so rock solid. Oddly, he made her feel wobbly, as if she needed a guy like him to save her.

I can save myself, she thought.

But she couldn't save herself. She picked up a guy who fucked her like crazy and then stole her car and went AWOL. In front of her mother, her sister, and Mr. Knight-in-Shining-Armor.

Finally the slick black rock appeared in front of her. She pulled herself up onto it and dropped back on the sun-warmed surface. She was spent, every muscle exhausted.

"You beat me," Brody said, and he piked his body up, spun around and sat on the edge of the rock.

"I so didn't beat you," Nell said, unmoving.

"You all right?" he asked.

"No," she said.

"Tired or something more serious?"

Nell didn't answer for a moment, considering all the possibilities. Tired. Sad. Angry. Embarrassed. How about crazy? Conjuring up a dead boyfriend was pretty wacky business.

Brody put his hand on her foot. "Rest for a while," he said.

But she couldn't rest. Her mind raced, thoughts colliding into each other. She and Chaney used to play a game, What Lurks in Your Brain, telling each other random thoughts that led to other random thoughts, the crazier the better, until they'd both be laughing hysterically. Why was everything so funny back then? Did he have a secret life of random thoughts that were dark and scary? Did she seem too frivolous a girlfriend to carry the burden of what really lurked in his brain?

Nell opened her eyes and stared at the sky. Wispy clouds sped across the expanse of pale blue. The sun warmed her body from above; the rock warmed her from below. She felt Brody's hand holding her foot as if he was scared she'd escape. Where the hell would I go?

"Your wife died, right?" Nell said, still staring above her into the endless sky.

And just like that he let go of her foot. She felt adrift somehow.

"Breast cancer," Brody finally said.

She sat up and looked at him. He gazed down into the water.

"I thought they could cure breast cancer these days."

"Not all kinds."

"Was she sick for a long time?"

Brody finally turned toward her. His face was different—

stonier, somehow. He didn't want to talk about it. No one wanted to talk about dead people.

He nodded. "A year."

"I wonder if that's easier," Nell said.

"Easier than what?" His voice was sharp.

"Than what Chaney did. Dying in an instant. Dying without letting me know."

Brody turned away but his hand wrapped around her foot again. She lay down, took a deep breath and felt herself sink into the rock as if her body could lose its hard edges.

"None of it's easy," Brody said. "Losing someone you love."

"But you had time to get used to the idea."

He shook his head. "There's no getting used to it." He tilted his head up to the sky. "And then she was gone."

Nell thought about all of the ways in which Chaney was gone. The funky smell of him when he came back from karate and she'd say: "Don't take a shower, take me to bed." The sound of his voice reading for the part of a frog in an animated movie. Later that night he croaked to her: "Wanna join me on my lily pad?" She still had his peacoat, which she wore every day of the mild Los Angeles winter even though it made her look a little homeless, a little childish. No, he was gone, gone, gone.

"I never told Chaney I loved him," she said quietly.

"Why not?"

"I was scared he'd flee. Guys do that. They're scared of girls like me."

"Why?"

"I wanted so much. Too much."

"There are guys who will want that."

She shook her head. "If Chaney had known that I loved him," she said finally, "he might not have killed himself."

"You couldn't save him, Nell."

"How do you know?"

"Because in the end, love isn't always enough."

She heard a shout and lifted her head. A kayak overturned near the rock and two teenagers screamed at each other in French.

"So how'd you do it?" she asked.

He glanced back at her, confused.

"Fall in love again."

"It's all your mother's fault," he said and he squeezed her foot.

"But you were ready," she said.

He looked out to sea. Finally he shook his head. "No, not ready," he said. "But you do it anyway. You fall again. You fall hard. You fall like you've never fallen in love before."

Nell felt tears on her face. She wanted to rest on the rock, Brody's hand on her foot, until the sun swept across the sky, until the others came looking for them, until it was time to go back to the inn and start again.

Later, Nell sat with her mother on the pebbly beach, watching the others swim.

"I can't believe Carly would blow off the kayaking trip," Olivia said.

"Give it a rest, Mom."

"It's just not like her."

Nell and Carly had an ongoing battle about their childhood. Nell was sure that her younger sister got all the attention: for her perfect grades, her science-fair inventions, her awards and her scholarships. Carly argued that Nell got all the attention every time she broke the rules, got caught, did it again. Olivia insisted that life wasn't fair—sometimes one kid took up all the space, sometimes the other one did. Get over it. There's enough love to go around.

So now Carly finally did something that should have pissed off her mother, and she was still getting all the attention. Nell felt like growling.

"So Carly needed a break," she said. "Who cares?"

"Brody cares," Olivia said. "He spent a lot of time planning this outing."

"And we're all loving it," Nell insisted.

"Carly won't give him a chance," Olivia said.

Nell shrugged. "She's a daddy's girl."

"Fine. It's great that she loves her father. Brody isn't competing for that role."

"Mom," Nell said. "Give her time. You can't make us into your new perfect little family in one weekend."

Olivia threw herself back on the beach, sighing loudly. "Why not?" she moaned.

"You're impossible," Nell said, finally offering her a smile.

"I'm glad to see you having fun," Olivia said, lifting her head.

"It's France," Nell said. "It's illegal to be unhappy in the south of France."

She patted her mother's leg, then stood up and started walking along the beach. She passed a family perched on the rocks, sharing a picnic. Someone's boom box blasted music. "I Wanna Sex You Up." One kid stood up and sang the song along with the recording, his strongly accented English making the words sound comical, his hips jutting from side to side. The mom laughed, the sister threw a grape at him. Everyone cracked up.

Gavin flitted into her mind again. *Has your sister ever had a boyfriend who is good enough for her?* Why was he so interested in Carly?

Don't think about Gavin. He's long gone. He's got a pretty French girl in the seat beside him and his hand's inching up her thigh.

Nell kept walking. At the end of the beach she saw two teenage boys sharing a joint. They stared at her, their eyes half-closed, their skinny bodies stretched out on the rocks. One of them pumped his hand near his crotch. Was he asking for a hand job? She turned around, disgusted.

"Mademoiselle!" one of them called.

She shook her head and kept walking.

Soon one of the boys was at her side, smelling of suntan lotion and sweat. He walked next to her as if he knew her, as if she had invited him for a stroll on the beach. He was her height but young, maybe thirteen or fourteen. He had a sly grin, long wavy hair, cat eyes. He'd be a lady-killer one day. Right now he was a punk.

"Leave me alone," she told him. But he didn't seem threatening. Just young.

"T'es américaine," he said. "I am sorry for my brother."

He pointed back toward the other boy on the rocks. The lewd one with his hand now curled beside his crotch, a reminder of what he wanted. He was older, she guessed. A tough guy.

"You speak English," she said. This brother was fine-boned, copper-colored.

He looked down, suddenly shy.

"T'es jolie," he said, raising his eyes.

"Merci," she told him.

"You want marijuana?" he asked, suddenly an eager puppy.

She laughed. "No," she said. "But I'd take a beer if you've got one."

He looked at her, confused. Too many words, too fast.

"Une bière?" she asked.

He ran back to the rocks, his body electric. In a mad dash, he scrambled through their cooler, found a beer, raced back to her side. All the while his brother watched her with heavy eyelids, his tongue traveling slowly across his lower lip.

"Merci," she said when the boy handed her the cold bottle.

"Une fête," he said breathlessly. "A party *ce soir. Tu viens avec moi?"*

She thought of the song "Lady Marmalade." *"Voulez-vous coucher avec moi ce soir."* She laughed. His face darkened.

She raised her beer to him. "I'm busy tonight. But thanks."

"Non?"

She shook her head. *"Non. T'as quel âge?"*

"Dix-huit ans." He was lying. No way this lovely boy-child was eighteen.

"All those people over there?" she said, pointing to the far edge of the beach where she could see her mother, Brody, and Fanny standing and talking. *"Ma famille,"* she said. *"Un mariage demain."*

She knew some French, but now only random words seemed to come to her in sudden bursts.

"Ton mariage?" he asked, looking painfully disappointed.

"Non," she said. *"Ma mère. Moi, je suis célibataire."* Single.

I'm single. Solo. All alone. His eyes brightened as if she had flicked the switch.

"Tarek," he said. "My name Tarek."

"Nell," she told him.

He leaned forward and kissed her gently on one cheek, then the other, his lips brushing her skin. "*Bonjour,* Nell," he said. His smile stretched across his face.

"I'll meet you here in ten years," she said in rapid-fire English. "How's that for a plan?"

"*Je ne comprends pas,*" he said, his brow furrowed in concentration.

"So which of you is the real bad-boy brother?" she asked. "The sleazy guy on the rocks or you, sweet-talking me like this?"

"*En français,*" he begged.

"I'm only allowed one stranger a weekend," she told him. "Already had as much fun as a girl could have with the first one. But man, are you cute."

"*Trop vite,*" he said. Too fast. Slow down.

But she was already moving on. At the other end of the beach her mother was waving madly to her. Nell took a long gulp of the beer and handed the boy the bottle. Then she leaned forward and kissed him on the lips. His eyes widened.

"*Au revoir, mon amour,*" she said.

And she walked away.

Chapter Twelve

Gavin sped along the winding mountain road, tires screeching around curves.

"Are we in a rush?" Carly asked.

"We've got all the time in the world," he said.

"Where are we going?" she finally asked. She had swallowed her fear when he turned away from Cassis and headed up into the hills. She didn't like fear. Back home, when she gave a speech in front of hundreds of people, she was cool, unflappable. Before then, exams were effortless, job interviews merely an interesting challenge. Even in high school, when she interned at Google and sat in on a meeting with Sergey, she didn't break a sweat. He asked her a question and she nailed it.

But this guy, her big sister's one-night stand, unnerved her. Or maybe she was thrown off by her own behavior. A

change in plans. A wild adventure with a stranger. It made her
heart thrum in her chest.

The hills were covered in a carpet of vineyards, the morning mist settling in the vines. They drove with the windows
half-open and she could smell wet dog. Had there been a dog
in the car?

"We'll go to Marseille," he said.

"What's in Marseille?"

"We'll find out," he said.

"We should be back for lunch," she told him.

"But you don't want to be," Gavin said, eyeing her.

"You're right," she said, and relief spread through her. She
didn't want to spend the day with her mother and her sister and
all those people. She remembered her promise to Sébastien. *I
plan on being completely immature.* Was it possible? Could she
spend a day without a plan?

Oddly, her mind settled on a memory: She and Nell were
walking along the Embarcadero with their father. They were
little—seven and nine, perhaps. Nell kept running ahead and
back like a hyperactive puppy. Each time she'd circle back
she'd try to steal Carly's scarf, a new striped scarf that her
mother had bought for her birthday. Carly kept swatting Nell's
hand away. She felt agitated, close to tears. She wanted her
father to yell at Nell, to tell her to stop pestering her. But her
father was telling a long story about why he chose to become a
lawyer and why Carly should be a lawyer. It had something to
do with the love of a logical mind, but she couldn't understand
what that meant. She didn't want him to think that something
as stupid as a scarf could ruin a wonderful day. And then the
scarf was gone, pulled from her neck in an instant, a sneak at-

tack from behind. She was sobbing, unable to move forward, and Nell was gone, the scarf wrapped tightly around her own neck. "What is it now?" her father said, with disgust. And then she realized: He didn't like children very much. He was waiting for her to grow up and in the meantime she'd have his love and attention as long as she acted like a grown-up and not a child. But she couldn't help herself; she railed against Nell, against the lost scarf, against the demands on her seven-year-old self.

Even then, she knew too much. She knew that Nell was a child and she was something else: a fraud, an impostor, a spy from the land of adults.

"We'll blow off lunch at the inn," Carly said boldly.

"If anyone complains, you can just say that I kidnapped you." Gavin offered her a half-smile; he glanced again at her legs.

She pressed the back of her hand against the window, expecting cool glass. But it was already hot outside. It was hot inside. Why didn't he turn on the air-conditioning?

"Does my sister know that you're gone?" Carly asked.

He lifted his eyebrows. "She's sleeping."

She thought of the sounds of sex all night long. Could that be the smell? He didn't take a shower. He was the wet dog in the hot car. She put her head back on the seat and closed her eyes. I don't know what happens next, she thought.

"Where's your boyfriend?" Gavin asked.

"In a meeting right now. In two or three meetings. On conference calls with four or five countries. In negotiations with five or six companies." She kept her eyes closed, smiling.

"Busy man," Gavin said.

"And I'm driving to Marseille with a stranger," Carly murmured.

"Your sister wanted to know me. You'd rather not know me."

She looked at him. He was right. She didn't want to know where he came from, where he went to college. Did he go to college? She didn't want the stories of his scars, his tattoos, his tortured past. And yet, she wanted this: to drive in the car with him, too fast. To turn the corner and see something she'd never seen before. To end up in Marseille because she had no notion of what would happen there.

They turned the corner and the sea appeared, the shade of blue startlingly bright.

"Tell me one thing about you," she said. "One astonishing thing."

He was quiet for a while and she scanned the horizon. A few fishing boats out to sea, one enormous cruise ship, a whisper of clouds in the distance. A perfect day for an adventure.

"Once I tell a lie," he finally said, "it becomes a truth. From that moment on, there is nothing truer in the world than that lie."

"And can you remember if it's a truth or a lie the next time you tell it?" she asked, watching him.

"No," he said. "The lie disappears forever."

She nodded. She was a truth-teller. Even in business she didn't believe in lies. Wes told her once that she'd beat everyone else because the rest of the world spent all their time covering up their lies.

So what does it mean to tell a lie and then believe it for the rest of your life? Something flickered at the edge of her memory. Nell. The high school dance. The police.

"And you?" Gavin asked. "One astonishing thing."

"I'd like to kiss you," she said.

Chapter Thirteen

Olivia needed to shower and change—her damp bathing suit clung to her skin. But Emily and Paolo were at work in the kitchen, conjuring up dishes that smelled like summer. She wanted to help; she wanted to make sure that Emily was weathering the marital storm.

"Take this to the outdoor table," Emily ordered, pushing a tray of wineglasses into Olivia's hands and ushering her out the door. "Nell—you grab the dishes. Out with you both."

So mother and daughter walked around the wooden trestle table under the arbor, setting the table for lunch. Emily had already laid out pale blue place mats and yellow cloth napkins. A row of shot glasses filled with sprays of wildflowers lined the center of the table.

"Imagine living like this every day," Olivia said.

"You'd go nuts," Nell told her. "You need chaos in your life."

"I do not," she argued. "My life isn't chaos."

"There's a blowup at the theater every day," Nell said. "You feast on that."

"Wrong," Olivia said. "I smooth out the ruffles. I want my life to look like this." She spread out her arms. The arbor sat at the edge of the meadow, with the pool and the field of wildflowers stretching beyond them. Terraced vineyards encircled the property and off to one side was a forest of pine trees.

"Well, it does feel good," Nell said. "This place settles the soul."

Olivia eyed her daughter. She was showered, her hair tousled. She wore cut-off jean shorts and a black tank top and looked as if she could be eighteen rather than twenty-eight. But even without makeup, this freshly scrubbed version of Nell looked vaguely dangerous. As if trouble would find her even if she didn't start it herself.

"What's that on your wrist?" Olivia asked as Nell set a bowl on the table. A purple oval bruise, the size of a thumbprint, colored the underside of her wrist.

Nell glanced at it and then shoved her hand in her pocket. "It's nothing," she said.

"Did Gavin do that?" Olivia asked.

"Of course not."

Olivia remembered the sounds coming from the bedroom in the middle of the night. Maybe they weren't sounds of rapture. Maybe he beat up her daughter and fled in the morning. "Nell, what did he do?"

Nell dropped into a chair at the table, sighing. "It's not a big deal."

"What's not a big deal?" Olivia could hear her heart pounding in her temples.

"He likes rough sex."

"What?"

"It doesn't mean anything," Nell said. "A lot of guys like that sort of thing."

"Nell," Olivia said, lowering her voice.

Nell looked away and her mouth dropped open. Olivia followed her glance and saw Jake standing at the opposite end of the table.

"Please go away," Olivia said, trying to keep her voice even.

"I'd like to help if I can," Jake said. Was he smiling? Olivia felt her stomach clench with anger.

"The table is set." She glared at him until he walked away, heading around the side of the house.

"Mom," Nell said quietly. "Drop it. Please."

"I can't drop it."

"Guys think girls like that sort of thing," Nell said.

"Do you?" Olivia asked.

"No." Nell toyed with a bracelet on her wrist, some kind of woven band with brightly colored beads. "I mean, he was sexy. Do we have to talk about this?"

"No. Yes." Olivia wanted to flee to the kitchen but she forced herself to stand there.

"He was sweet, too," Nell said. "He was rough and then he was really gentle. I told him I liked him better when he was gentle."

"Good," Olivia said. She felt as if she were talking to a ten-year-old version of her daughter, not this sex kitten perched on a chair.

"I need a shower," Olivia said. "And food. I'd also like it if your sister joined us this weekend." She walked away, her body radiating anger. Was she angry at Gavin? No. She was furious at her daughter.

As she stepped into the kitchen she looked back. Nell's face was lifted to the sun. One hand leisurely stroked the bruise on her wrist. Olivia watched for a moment, transfixed. Does my daughter choose pain? she thought as she closed the door.

"You are bride," a voice said.

She spun around. Paolo stood next to the center island, holding a quiche in his mitted hands. He looked young and sweet and fresh from the oven.

"I am bride," Olivia said, smiling.

"I am happy for you," he told her.

"Thank you. Shall I take that to the table?"

"No, you are bride," he said.

"I'm an old bride," she told him. "I can do kitchen duty and get married all in the same weekend."

"It is very good weekend. Wedding. Family. You are, how you say . . ."

"Lucky," Olivia said. "Happy. Grateful. Yes. Thank you."

"Why do you thank me?"

"For reminding me."

"I don't understand."

"How old are you?"

"Twenty-eight."

"Do you have a wife? A girlfriend?"

He shook his head. "Soon," he said.

"I hope so," she told him.

Emily walked into the kitchen, carrying bottles of wine. "Oh, that's gorgeous, Paolo." She took in a deep breath of quiche and then glanced at Olivia. "Go take your shower. Lunch will be served in ten minutes."

Olivia saluted. "I'm lucky," she said. "I'm lucky and happy and grateful."

"And a little crazy," Emily said. "Go. Now. Or we'll eat without you."

"*Grazie,*" she whispered to Paolo on her way out of the kitchen.

Olivia heard the shower running when she walked into her room. She pulled off her bathing suit, grabbed a bathrobe from the chair and wrapped it around her. Holding her cellphone, she dropped onto the bed, suddenly exhausted.

She tapped onto Carly's name. It went right to voice mail. She tossed the phone onto the pillow.

"Nap time?" Brody asked.

She lifted her head. He was standing in the middle of their room, a towel wrapped around his waist. Steam poured in from the open door of the bathroom. His hair was wet, his body still damp.

"Why do people have rough sex?" Olivia asked.

"Who has rough sex?"

"No one," Olivia said. "I'm just curious."

"I'm not really into that kind of thing," Brody said gently, sitting on the edge of the bed.

"Is it a control thing? One person has to have the power?"

"Is this the big conversation before we get married? This is when you bring out your whips and chains?"

"Are you scared?"

"Very."

Olivia rolled toward him and put her hand on his bare back. "I'm worried about my girls. I don't understand them. Nell comes prancing in with some brute. Who knows, maybe Carly's out looking for sex right now."

"Who cares if she is?" Brody said. "She's an adult. She can do what she wants. Maybe she ran off with Gavin this morning."

"What?" Olivia heard the screech in her voice. "What are you talking about?"

"Maybe she went for a hayride with the guy. This is our wedding weekend. Can we forget about your girls for one minute and think about us?"

Olivia stood up. Too many words jumbled in her brain. She spun around, opened the door, and walked out. She slammed the door behind her.

Jake stood in the hallway, a crooked smile on his face.

"Fuck you," she said and she stormed past him.

Chapter Fourteen

Nell's cellphone buzzed in her pocket. She pulled it out.

Wesley Keller. Carly's boyfriend. She was surprised she had his number logged in her phone. Then she remembered that she had called Wes once, when she was planning a surprise for Carly. She'd arranged for an actor friend to show up at Carly's office on her birthday. He sang a jazzy version of "Happy Birthday" while performing a striptease—Carly kicked him out before he had his pants off. She never even called Nell to thank her.

She calculated the time—two in the afternoon in France meant five in the morning, a Saturday morning, in California. What the hell?

She walked to one end of the pool and dropped into a lounge chair.

"Hello?"

"Nell, it's Wes."

"Yeah, I know. Early out there."

"I've been trying to reach Carly. She's not answering her phone." He sounded alert and clear. Who are these people who can function at five in the morning?

"She disappeared. Poof. Gone."

"What?"

Nell enjoyed his confusion. When she first met him, at a birthday party for her mother in San Francisco, he asked her what her goals were in life. To drink well, she said. To eat well. To have great sex. He watched her for the rest of the evening as if through the bars of a cage. Species from another planet. Don't get too close.

"She took off by herself this morning," she told Mr. Clean now. "Walk on the beach, that kind of thing."

"Without her phone?" he asked.

"Maybe. That so weird?"

"She doesn't go anywhere without her phone. It's going right to voice mail. She never turns off her damn phone."

"It probably died. Mine always dies."

"Carly's phone never dies," he said impatiently.

"Right. She probably charges it all the time." Nell laughed nervously. "Can't help you, Wes. I'm not my sister's keeper."

"I thought you might—"

"You broke your leg," Nell said, suddenly remembering.

"What?"

"Carly told me that you broke your leg. At dinner last night. It was one of the first things she told me."

"I didn't break my leg."

"Skydiving."

"That's ridiculous."

"Carly doesn't lie."

"I do not skydive."

"So why would she say that?"

"Maybe she was trying to get your attention."

Nell stood up and walked into the grove of trees at the edge of the meadow. The wind had picked up and the trees rustled above her. Hansel-and-Gretel land. Where was the witch? Where was the cottage with the cage and the oven?

"She thinks I don't pay attention to her?" Nell asked, her voice quiet.

"Maybe you should talk to *her* about it," Wes said.

Nell walked toward an opening in the trees and found a vegetable garden filled with a bounty of plants. Green beans, tomatoes, cucumbers, peppers, kale, lettuces of every color. She reached for a cherry tomato and popped it into her mouth. The juices exploded on her tongue. Carly wanted her attention? I'd give her anything she wants, she thought.

"I talked to her yesterday," Wes said, his voice soft in her ear. "It was the middle of the night there."

"Where was she?"

"In her hotel room. Listening to you have sex with some guy."

"Oh. Awkward, huh."

"She was in a strange mood," Wes told her.

"How so?"

"She was mad at me for not coming."

"That doesn't sound so strange."

"She was sad. Lonely."

Nell imagined her little sister at a cocktail party in Silicon Valley, hordes of people gathered around her, all of them wanting to get close to the whiz kid. How could Carly be lonely?

"She seemed okay at dinner."

"Yeah, well, she's good at hiding that sort of thing," Wes said.

Nell felt something well up in her chest and she pressed her hand there, willing it to subside.

A couple of birds flew from the branches ahead, creating a flurry of noise and motion. Something dropped in front of her—a bird's egg!

She stared at it, broken at her feet. It was vivid blue, impossibly small. Something oozed from the side of the broken shell.

"Give me your mother's number," Wes said. "I'll call her."

"No," Nell said, her voice suddenly loud. "I'll take care of this. My mother is crazed. Don't call her."

He didn't say anything.

"Really, Wes," Nell said, trying to make her voice calm and contained. "I'll tell Carly to call you as soon as she gets back."

"Tell her—" Wes started. Then he went silent. Nell shivered as the sun moved behind a cloud.

"Listen," she said. "I'm losing service. I'm in the woods near the inn and I can't hear you very well." It wasn't true. She felt some kind of panic coming on. She needed to do something and she didn't have any idea what that would be.

"I can hear you just fine," Wes said.

"What? I can't hear you. Listen. I'll keep you posted. I'm sure she'll be back soon. Don't worry. And I'm glad you didn't break your leg."

She hung up before he could say anything else.

She sat on the ground, resting her back against a tree.

What happened to Little Red Riding Hood when she walked through the woods? Nell tried to recall the story. Little Red saw a wolf dressed up as her grandma. He tried to eat her. She closed her eyes and listened to the roar of the wind in the trees.

Later, Nell set jugs of water on the outdoor table. Emily had already carried out platters of cheese and salami and olives. There was a tomato and mozzarella salad and a spinach quiche, both artfully presented on beautiful Provençal plates.

"I hear we've got a mistral headed our way," Emily said, emerging from the kitchen with a large ceramic bowl in her hands. She placed sautéed haricots verts, sprinkled with salt and garlic, in the center of the table. Jake stood at one end, opening bottles of rosé.

"What's that?" Nell asked.

"That's our regional windstorm. They say it brings out the crazy in everyone."

"Just what we need," Nell said.

"What happens if it rains tomorrow?" Jake asked. "On the wedding day."

"Let's not talk about it," Olivia said, walking toward them with a basket of bread.

"The rain or the wedding?" Jake asked, raising an eyebrow.

Olivia slammed the breadbasket onto the table.

"Can I pour you a glass of wine?" he offered into the silence.

"I'd love one," Nell said, but he poured Olivia a glass. Olivia took it and turned her back on all of them.

"Can I have some wine?" Nell asked, feeling like the invisible child. Carly used to complain about Olivia when they were teenagers. Don't you hate it? she'd say after a dinner party when the sisters would lie in their twin beds. "Everyone loves her," Nell would say, feeling pride about her mother's magnetic power. "She takes up all the space in the room," Carly would snipe.

Nell liked living far away from her sister and her start-up in Silicon Valley, her mother and her theater company in San Francisco, her father and his very-big-deal law firm. Nell strived for her own small life. Unlike many of the struggling actors she knew, she didn't dream of stardom. She dreamt of small roles in films. Now she dreamt of getting a gig teaching yoga at Om Studios in Santa Monica. She couldn't fail if she kept her ambition pint-sized.

Jake filled her wineglass. When she looked up at him he winked.

She grimaced. Leave me alone, old man.

She walked away from all of them, heading back toward the house, wine in hand. When she pushed open the kitchen door, she saw Paolo at the center island, whipping something in a large white bowl.

"Dessert?" she asked.

"*Sì,*" he said. He looked at her and then looked out the windows toward the arbor. "Your sister. She is, how you say . . ." His brow furrowed in concentration.

"Flew the coop," Nell said. "Runaway child."

He looked confused.

"You know what I'm going to do?" she asked, and he shook

his head. She needed to learn to speak more slowly. She needed to learn new languages. "I'm going to go find her."

His eyes brightened.

"Good idea, huh," she said. "What's a wedding party without a sister or two?"

He put the bowl down on the counter. "You are different sister."

"I am different sister. You got that right, my friend."

She walked over to him. He looked a little scared. She reached her finger into the bowl and dipped it into a mound of whipped chocolate. Then she slipped her finger into her mouth.

"Save me some," she said. "I'll be dreaming about this chocolate all day."

He nodded though she was sure he had no idea what she was saying.

She dipped her finger into the bowl again. This time she used the chocolate to write a message on the center island.

A la plage!

Paolo squinted at the words. He held the bowl, wrapped in his arms, protecting the rest from her greedy fingers.

"*Ciao,*" she said.

"*Ciao,*" he repeated uncertainly.

She walked out the back door, straight past her mother, past Emily and Jake chatting it up at the table. She waited for someone to stop her. For her mother to tell her to sit down and eat lunch with them. She'd think her a fool for searching for her sister. Carly takes care of Carly.

But no one said a word as she walked across the lawn, around the house and down the driveway to the street below.

Chapter Fifteen

Gavin pushed Carly back against the wall of a building, pressing his lips into hers.

She felt his tongue probing her mouth, hard, insistent. No, she thought. This isn't what I want. She pushed against his chest.

"You asked me to kiss you," Gavin said. His lips were wet, his eyes cloudy.

"Not yet," Carly said.

"You're a tease," he told her. He still held her shoulders pressed against the cold stone wall.

"Maybe a girl wants a little romance first," she said.

He shook his head, his eyes on her. "You don't want romance."

She felt her heart thudding inside her head. Don't show fear. Don't give him that power over you.

Carly saw garbage flying through the street, airborne on a gust of wind. She heard French rap music blasting from an apartment window.

"Show me Marseille," she said. "I'll kiss you when I'm ready."

He released her and walked away.

Let him go, she thought. You don't need him.

A plastic bag blew in the wind and tangled on her arm. She shook it off and saw a smear of something red across her arm. She grabbed a Kleenex from her purse and wiped the smear off. Ketchup. Not blood.

She caught up with Gavin and fell into step beside him.

"I don't like it here," she said.

"You wanted an adventure," he told her.

"There must be an old part of the city. Something charming."

"This is Marseille," he said.

"The port! Let's walk to the port."

Gavin stopped and turned to her. "I'm not a tourist guide."

"I know that."

"Do you want a good time?"

Sex, she thought. He's talking about sex. She thought about Wes, his pale body hovering above hers, his slim penis sliding in and out of her. He always looked so serious while making love, as if he were taking an exam that he might not ace.

Nell never said no to a good time. She learned to ride a motorcycle when she was sixteen. At seventeen, she went to

Burning Man with a bunch of guys she met in Dolores Park. She drove to Las Vegas with a casting director who left her there after two days and nights of partying.

Do I want a good time?

Not sex, she thought. Something else, something that will take me someplace new.

"Yes," she said.

"Good girl," he said.

He started walking again, and she hurried to keep at his side.

They entered a plaza encircled by shops and cafés. A fenced playground stretched across the middle of the open space. Two women wearing hijabs watched their children on the swings. An older Arab man, blind, made his way across the courtyard, banging on garbage cans, street signs and café chairs with his white-tipped cane.

Her mother and sister were probably kayaking in the brilliant blue sea right now. Maybe they were back at the inn, having lunch in the garden. She thought of fields of lavender, stretching as far as the eye could see. Vineyards, ripe with grapes glistening in the hot sun. A white sand beach, the sea-washed pebbles cool under her feet.

A man walked by her, his eyes on her breasts.

Carly slipped her arm through Gavin's.

Her sister's guy. Her mother's wedding weekend. Go back. Leave him.

Gavin pressed her arm against his side. She could smell him. Some odd mixture of sex and sandalwood.

Wes had no smell. He wore no cologne. After work, after

exercise, after sex, he took a shower. He didn't push her against the wall of a building and kiss her.

She remembered visiting Nell in L.A. once during a trip with her high school debate team. Nell took her to a bar at night, supplying her with a friend's ID. Carly drank a glass of white wine but Nell drank scotch, one after another. A couple of guys came over and asked them to dance. Carly had a boyfriend; she said no. "He's not asking you to marry him," Nell whispered. "Have a little fun." But she sat alone on a bar stool, texting the boyfriend back in San Francisco. Nell danced for an hour or two, with both guys, with everyone on the dance floor. And when they walked back to Nell's apartment, late at night, Carly could smell her sister's booze and sweat and joy. The next day the boyfriend dumped her for her best friend. She won the debate championship.

Have a little fun.

Do you want a good time?

Gavin turned a corner, keeping her close, her arm tight against his body. He whispered in her ear, "Little sister." She could feel his warm breath on her neck.

"Where are we going?" she asked. Her voice sounded like someone else's voice. Afraid. Unsure.

"You'll see," he said.

Chapter Sixteen

Emily and Olivia were the last two left at the outdoor table under the arbor. The salad platters were almost empty; the wine was gone. Fanny had retired to take a nap, Sébastien went to fix a broken table in the library, and Jake was swimming laps in the pool behind them.

Brody never came down to lunch. Olivia told herself that he was napping, but she knew that she was supposed to fetch him and offer an apology. Still, she didn't move.

"You can't be mad at Nell because she likes rough sex," Emily said. She leaned back and put her feet up on the chair beside her.

"You look exhausted," Olivia said.

"You're not listening to me."

"I am." She, too, slumped back in her chair. She closed her

eyes in the bright sunlight. The warm wind seemed to slow the world down.

"It's not such a horrible thing," Emily said.

"Oh my God," Olivia said, sitting up suddenly, and staring at her friend. "You like rough sex?"

"Not really rough sex. But some stuff. Tying each other up. That sort of thing."

Olivia shook her head. "I don't think I want to know this." She put her head back on her chair.

"I wouldn't talk about it. Normally. But you're mad at Nell and you shouldn't be."

Olivia didn't like it when her best friend told her how to deal with her daughters. It was so easy to give advice about child-rearing when you weren't a parent.

"I *am* mad at Nell. But it's not about the rough sex."

"I don't think being mad at her right now makes any sense."

"Who said I'm making sense?"

"Why are you mad at her?"

Olivia dropped her head on the table. When she lifted it, she looked at Emily. "There's something so vulnerable about Nell. I saw it today. I can imagine why men take advantage of her. She doesn't protect herself. She's too raw."

"She's young."

"We were never like that when we were young. Carly's not like that."

"Carly's not like anyone."

"Do you know what I'm talking about?" Olivia asked.

Emily nodded. "She doesn't have the mettle that you and Carly have. So you need a little more compassion with her."

"I need a little more wine."

Emily reached for the bottle. "We finished it," she said. "I'll get more."

"No. I have to be sober. I'm getting married tomorrow."

Emily got up and walked around the table. She sat in the chair next to Olivia and took her hand.

"About a minute ago," Emily said, "we were two kids in a dorm room at Berkeley. I'd give anything to be back there in time."

"Not a chance in hell," Olivia said. "I was an idiot. I thought I was God's gift to acting. I thought I'd travel around the world with a backpack and a good stash of drugs for ten years."

"I thought I could trust love," Emily said.

Olivia squeezed her hand. "Have you guys talked any more?"

"I don't want to," she said. "I don't believe him. I don't understand him."

"He fucked up," Olivia said. "In a big way."

"Here's the crazy part. In France an affair just isn't a big deal. Everyone does it."

"That can't really be true."

"I think it's true," Emily said. "Sébastien's friends have flings all the time. His mother had a paramour who came to her funeral. The young girl who cleans for me here has a married lover who pays for her apartment. Apparently, he buys two of everything. Two sexy nightgowns, one for her and one for his wife. Two bouquets of irises. Two gold necklaces with starfish pendants."

"Is that what Sébastien is arguing? That it's no big deal?"

Emily shook her head. "He knows it's a big deal. For us it's a big deal."

"Somehow you guys have to get past this."

"Why?"

"Because you love him?"

Emily shrugged. "You get to a certain point in a marriage when you don't even know what love is anymore. You live together, you take care of each other, your lives become inter-twined. But love? Big old passionate love? I'm not sure I re-member that kind of love."

"It evolves. At least I think it does. What do I know? Mac and I went from love to boredom in a flash. We skipped those steps: taking care of each other, intertwining our lives. We lived parallel lives. And suddenly we couldn't care less about each other."

"And it's different with Brody?" Emily asked.

"Brody and I will do it differently," Olivia said. Can I do it differently? she thought. Yes. This is grown-up love. I'm dif-ferent than I was at twenty-six. "We'll take care of each other," she told Emily. "We'll wrap our lives around each other."

"But you have work. He doesn't."

Olivia stood up. "Now I'm getting more wine." She walked toward the house, carrying two empty bottles with her.

"And chocolate!" Emily shouted after her. "There's a box of salted caramels on the counter."

Olivia stepped into the kitchen and saw Brody at the sink, staring out the window.

"I thought you were napping," she said.

"Did you come to look for me?" he asked.

Olivia shook her head. "I'm sorry." She reached out and placed her hand on the small of his back. "Come outside. We'll feed you."

Brody shook his head. "You and Emily are talking. I don't want to intrude."

"She just asked me about your not working."

"What about it?"

"Whether it causes us to live separate lives."

"What did you say?"

"I said I needed more wine."

"I *will* get a job," Brody said, a hint of defensiveness in his voice. "I'm not going to spend my day waiting for you to come home from work."

But that's what you're doing, she thought. It's been three months. And every day I come home you're waiting for me so you can start your life.

Olivia sat on a stool at the counter. She felt the weight of those evenings on her now. She would ask him about his day. He would describe a walk to Crissy Field, a day spent wandering the Presidio. And soon enough she would be telling him about her fight with the producer of the next play. The rave *Chronicle* review of the current play. The new playwright who was going to work with them next fall. Brody's face would open up as she told her stories. All day he's been waiting for me to come home, she thought.

"What if you can't find a job?" she asked.

Brody took a step back from her. "We'll be okay. I have money saved."

"It's not all about the money. You'll be lost without work. You love working."

"I'm taking a break from working. That's all."

Mac had been a workaholic. And Olivia threw herself into her projects with an intensity that dazzled most people. Carly's life was her work. What happens to a person who doesn't work?

She thought of a long rambling walk she and Brody had taken in Wyoming one day. Where are we going? she had asked. Everywhere, he told her. They walked for hours, through a great expanse of open land and unending sky. He named the snakes they saw; he spotted an eagle for her. She stopped looking at her watch, stopped thinking about tonight's dinner, tomorrow's flight home.

She looked up at Brody now. "I might learn something from you," she said. "About how to live instead of how to work."

His face softened and he pulled her toward him.

"I love you," she said quietly.

He leaned over and kissed her. His cellphone rang in his pocket. He glanced at it and then at Olivia.

"It's my dad," he said.

"Take it," Olivia told him.

Brody answered the phone and walked over to the tall kitchen windows.

"I'm here," he said into the phone. And then he listened for a long time. He sat on a stool by the center island and Olivia could see from the set of his shoulders that he was hearing bad news.

"There must be something you can do," Brody finally said.

He sat with the phone pressed against his ear for a long time. Olivia moved to a stool beside him, placing her hand on his thigh.

"You have to tell Mom," he said into the phone.

After a while, his voice got louder. "You can't do that, Dad," he said. "Let her help you."

Olivia saw his hand curl into a fist.

Finally he relaxed and spoke quietly into the phone. "I'll tell her. But you have to promise to let her take care of you."

When he hung up the phone, he was quiet and Olivia saw that he was crying. She stood up and put her arms around his shoulders.

"He's got cancer," Brody said, his voice quiet. "It's already in his liver."

"Oh, I'm so sorry," Olivia said, holding him.

Brody spoke through his tears. "That's why he moved out. He's the smartest man I know and he's an absolute idiot. He didn't want Mom to suffer while he died. He wanted to go away and do it by himself."

"He's changed his mind?" Olivia asked.

Brody nodded. "I think he got scared. Or guilty about missing the wedding. Or he just missed her. Damn fool. He couldn't spend a day without her and then he walks out on her because he thinks she's not strong enough to watch him die."

"He was the caretaker, the doctor," Olivia said. "Maybe he didn't believe anyone could take care of him."

Brody nodded. He wiped his face with the back of his hand.

"Bastard," he mumbled.

"We'll go out there when we get back," Olivia said.

Brody reached an arm out and pulled her close to him. "I've got to go tell my mother. She'll be devastated."

"But she'll get him back for a little while," Olivia said. "And she'll understand why he left her. The fool."

"Sorry, *mes amis,*" Sébastien said, walking into the kitchen. They broke apart and Brody swiped his eyes once again.

"I have some news from the police," Sébastien said.

"What?" Olivia asked.

"They found Nell's rental car in Marseille. It was parked in town. Illegally. Gavin must have left it there and moved on in some other way."

"What do we have to do?" Brody asked.

"*Rien,*" Sébastien said. "Hertz will get the car. The police do not care about pursuing Gavin."

"Good riddance to him," Olivia said.

"Where's Nell?" Brody asked.

Olivia pointed to the chocolate message on the center island.

A la plage!

"Remind me why we invited my daughters to our wedding?" Olivia asked, sliding her arm around Brody's back.

"Entertainment," Brody said. "The Sister Show."

"Any chance we can change the channel?"

Chapter Seventeen

Nell walked along the cafés that border the marina of Cassis. She had thought that she spotted her sister in the dark interior of one restaurant. But it turned out to be a French look-alike, a young woman who gave Nell the evil eye for circling her table. Now Nell focused on the pedestrians who filled the street, strolling in one direction or the other.

Most of them were tourists, she guessed. Sunburned and well fed, Germans and Americans, their bellies spilling over the tops of their shorts. The *quai* was crowded with them, speaking many different languages, long lines of them waiting for sightseeing boats that would take them to the calanques. Small groups of people stopped at each restaurant, reading the menus, discussing their choices. Nell could smell a heady mix of suntan lotion, perfume, and fish.

Carly was nowhere.

Maybe she saw Gavin leaving in the morning and decided to hitch a ride.

Ridiculous. Carly was too straight for the Gavins of the world. She liked her guys brilliant and boring, cut from the same mold as her dad. Nell never understood Carly's attraction to Mr. Clean. Power maybe. Money. But what do you end up with—nights in bed with a geek? Wes had no sex appeal, no passion except for the success of his company. Carly deserved better than that.

No, her sister wanted a day by herself. Still, there was something odd about it. Carly didn't break the rules.

Nell pulled her phone out of her pocket and called Carly's cell. Again, it went directly to voice mail.

"I'm worried about you, sister," she said. "Call me."

She could hear the shakiness in her own voice.

She had just turned eighteen. She had just gotten into UC Santa Cruz, her first choice. Finally, she was getting her shit together. She had broken up with Harper after he stole the Xanax and Vicodin from her mother's medicine cabinet. She had a 3.8 on her most recent report card, an improvement so shocking that her adviser asked her if she was cheating. She didn't tell the guy that she had stopped getting stoned on the way to school. That she liked her immigrant lit class and her creative writing class and read all the books she was assigned. She had a new friend at school, a fearless lesbian who taught her rock climbing. She was thinking about working in Mexico that summer, helping women in remote mountain villages build sustainable vegetable gardens. Her drama teacher had shown her the program brochure and she had already emailed for information.

For the first time in four years she decided to go to the high school dance. She'd go solo, she'd go straight, she'd see what the hell she had been missing all this time.

The gym was crowded and loud; it reeked of alcohol and hormones. She thought of the bag of weed she had stashed back at the house. She should have gotten stoned first. This was too crazy. She'd walk through once; then she'd go home and get high.

But she spotted Carly in the middle of the dance floor, turning in circles, her arms swaying above her head. She wasn't moving in time to the music. She had a serene smile on her face as if she were someplace far away from the pounding music and gyrating kids. Two boys danced around her, sometimes rubbing their bodies up against her.

Nell had never seen Carly dance like this. She remembered a cousin's wedding a year or so ago—Carly did an awkward hip shimmy and kept her arms pinned to her side. Geek dancing, Nell called it. This was something else.

She's high, Nell realized.

But Carly didn't smoke weed, didn't take pills. She was sixteen and unbearably straight. She thought people who smoked cigarettes were bad people.

So why was she dancing like that?

Nell walked around the dance floor, keeping an eye on her sister. Carly had gone to a friend's house before the dance. She and her friends always seemed to do things in large groups. Nell had never been a part of a group. She didn't understand the need to move in packs, to dress alike, to fill every room with so much noise. Where was Carly's pack? Nell knew some of the girlfriends—Elise, Brenna, Fern, Dina. She couldn't find any of them. She recognized one of the boys pressing his body against her sister. Rico. A senior like Nell. He got a girl pregnant last year; he was suspended for selling fake IDs this year. Nell moved closer to the center of the dance floor.

Rico ran his hand over Carly's breasts. Carly kept smiling and leaned her body into him.

"Rico!" Nell called out.

He didn't look at her. Carly twirled around and the other boy put his hands on her hips and then pressed her into him. His hands moved to her ass, holding her to him.

Nell stepped up and pushed him away. He stumbled back. Nell put her arm around Carly who wobbled on her high heels.

"What are you on?" she asked her sister.

"I'm fine," Carly said, still smiling.

"No, you're not."

"Leave her alone," Rico said. "We're having a good time."

"Not with you," Nell said.

"I wanna dance," Carly said, her words slurred. "It feels so good."

Her arms rose above her; her hips swung from side to side.

"You're high," Nell said. "You're fucked up. I'm taking you home."

"I am not," Carly said and she began to giggle.

"You think this is smart?" Nell asked. "You just won the Google internship. You're going to Seattle for the debate finals. You think this is how you're supposed to behave?"

"Who the hell are you to tell me how to behave?" Carly barked, her smile gone. She stopped swaying and put her hands on her hips.

"You jealous of her, Nell?" Rico taunted. "You wish you were dancing with me?"

He snaked his arm around Carly's waist and pulled her toward him. He leaned down and pressed his mouth into hers. Carly started to push back, her hands on his chest.

Nell kicked him hard in the shin. He let go of Carly for a moment and swung wildly toward Nell. The other guy who had been dancing with Carly grabbed his arm and shouted, "Fuck no. We ain't getting busted here, man."

Nell grabbed Carly's hand and led her through the crowd as quickly as she could. Carly stopped fighting her and kept close as they wove through the dancers.

"Do you have a jacket? A purse?" Nell called to her over the din.

Carly looked confused. And then she shouted, "Jacket!" She veered toward the bleachers and pulled her jean jacket off one of the benches. She passed it to Nell who tucked it under her arm.

They made their way to the doors and pushed through the crowd milling there. Once they were outside, Nell dragged Carly away from everyone else. They stood on the sidewalk; cars sped past them.

"Put this on," Nell said, throwing the jacket at Carly.

"I'm hot. I don't need it." The jacket fell to her feet.

"What are you on?" Nell asked.

"What do you care?" Carly shot back. "What are *you* on?"

"Is it E?"

"What's E?" Carly asked. She was swaying again, her arms swinging around her body.

"Ecstasy. Christ, Carly. What did you take?"

"I drank a little," she said.

Nell frowned. "You hate booze."

"Not anymore. I got too high and someone said to drink a few shots of tequila and then I felt so much better."

"Too high? What was it?"

"Some kind of pill. And if you tell Mom I'll murder you."

"I'm not telling anyone. I'm just getting you out of here."

"Why? I'm having so much fun."

"Freak dancing with that asshole? We're going home."

Nell grabbed the jacket from the ground and put it on. She took Carly's wrist and led her through the parking lot to her car.

"You're an idiot," Nell said when they got in the car.

"I feel sick," Carly said.

"If you're going to throw up, do it outside. Don't mess up my car."

Carly put her head back on the seat and closed her eyes. "Everybody left. I didn't know where they all went. But I didn't care. I started dancing and I didn't care about anything."

"Good for you," Nell said, starting the car.

"Good for me," Carly murmured, dreamily.

Nell looked at her sister as she pulled out of the parking lot. Carly was the smartest kid in the school. And now she was just another fucked-up teenager. "Go right to bed when we get home. Don't talk to Mom. I'll tell her you're sick. And don't text anyone. Just put on some music and veg out."

Carly smiled.

"You've never vegged out in your life," Nell said.

"Everything's so pretty out here," Carly said, peering out the front window.

"Man, are you fried."

And then the red flashing light appeared behind them. The siren filled the space of the car. Carly covered her ears and began to whimper.

"Fuck," Nell said. "I wasn't speeding. Don't get out of the car. No matter what. You sit right there. Do you hear me?"

"Yes," Carly said, her head in her hands.

"Don't talk to them. I'll deal with it."

Nell pulled the car over to the side of the road and got out of the car.

"Stay right where you are, young lady," the cop called out.

Nell shut the door behind her and leaned back against it. She shaded her eyes with her hand as she watched the two cops approach her. One man, one woman.

"I wasn't speeding," she said.

"Step away from the car," the male cop said. He had a booming voice that rang out in the dark night.

"I didn't do anything wrong."

The male cop walked up to her and the woman cop circled the car. She tapped her flashlight against her hip, as if waiting to hit someone.

"Big dance at the high school tonight," the male cop said.

"I'm just taking my sister home. She's sick."

"Has she been drinking?"

"No," Nell said. "She's got the flu or something."

"You been drinking?"

"No," Carly said. "I was there for like ten minutes. It sucked. We're going home."

"You rolled through that stop sign," the male cop said.

Nell looked back at the intersection. "No, I didn't," she said, but she wasn't sure.

The female cop opened the passenger door.

"Leave her alone," Nell said.

"Let's get her out of the car," the male cop said.

"She wasn't driving. Leave her alone!" Nell yelled. She dug her hands into the pockets of the jean jacket. Immediately she felt something round and hard: a pill bottle, she guessed.

"What's in your pocket?"

"Nothing," Nell said. "My hands are just cold." She pulled her hands out of her pockets.

The cop stepped closer to her, and patted her pocket, running his hand over the hard plastic.

"Give me your jacket," he said, his voice rough.

"No," Nell said. "I don't have to do that."

"Get the other girl out of the car," he yelled to his partner.

"She wasn't driving!" Nell yelled.

"Give me your jacket and we'll leave her alone," the cop told her.

Nell saw Carly try to step out of the car. She stumbled, then fell back, banging her head against the roof of the car.

Nell took off her jacket and tossed it to the cop.

"Just leave my sister out of it," she said. "She's got nothing to do with this."

The cop pulled the pill bottle out and looked inside.

"You're under arrest," he said.

———

Nell stopped at a café and ordered a *sandwich au fromage* and a *bière* to go. She spoke some French that she had learned from a French boyfriend. They had met at a weekend yoga retreat in Santa Barbara and had spent their time stretching their muscles in bed in her cabin rather than on the yoga mat. He was tall and skinny and had a wonderful uncircumcised penis that was as acrobatic as he was. When they both returned to L.A., she found out that he had a fiancée. So they saw each other on the sly for a while, always at Nell's apartment, always in bed. Never in public. Until the girlfriend found a text from her—*chez moi ce soir*—and the guy disappeared from her life. *Quel dommage.*

At least she had learned the language of love—or perhaps it was just the language of sex. He was good for that and a case of herpes.

She took her sandwich and beer and walked out to the lighthouse at the end of the breakwater. The wind had picked up, filling her ears with a rushing sound. The sea was topped with whitecaps. Most of the kayakers and sailboats were heading back to port.

She sat on a rock near the lighthouse, facing back to land. The houses along the harbor were painted in faded pastel colors with vibrant colored shutters on all the windows. It looked postcard perfect except for the sound of a police siren in the distance.

She pulled out her phone and scrolled through her contacts. She didn't know what she was looking for—someone to talk to. But Chaney was the only person she had ever really talked to. She had felt safe with Chaney; she felt like herself with him. With the French guy she was always trying to be the wild one, the girl who didn't ask for anything but a kiss before he slipped

out of her house. With her sister she was always trying to be
more sensible than she was, more focused on her career. When
she and Carly talked on the phone Nell would tell her about
the great auditions, the calls from her agent promising fabulous roles. She would never tell her that she drank too much
the night before and slept too late that morning.

But Chaney let her be whoever the hell she was. And he
seemed to want her just that way. Sometimes they hung out,
watching romantic comedies all night. At other times, on a
whim, they'd hop in the car and take off for Big Bear. Tijuana.
Joshua Tree. Life was a wild ride.

She clicked on one of the contacts on her iPhone. Lillian,
Chaney's mother. It was a crazy thing to do, calling her. She
should hang up. She barely knew Lillian.

But the phone was already ringing and she kept it held to
her ear.

"Hello?" the woman said, and Nell felt a jolt of joy. Chaney's
Mom.

"Lillian. Hi, it's Nell." She heard a silence. She thought of
hanging up—she'd never have to see the woman again,
anyway—but she pressed the phone to her ear.

"Nell. Why are you calling?"

Chaney's mother once told him she thought Nell was too
skinny. Had Lillian liked her? Nell didn't know. They had only
seen each other a few times in the year she and Chaney had
been together. And two times since he died: at the funeral and
at the apartment, when Lillian came to get Chaney's clothes.

"I was just thinking about Chaney," Nell said. "I was missing him."

"I miss him all the time," Lillian said, her voice soft.

"Had he talked about me very much?" Nell asked.

"What do you mean?"

"I'm trying to figure out if he loved me."

"I'm sure he loved you."

"I hope he did. I loved him. He's the only guy I've ever loved."

She could hear Lillian begin to cry.

"I don't want to upset you," Nell said.

"No," Lillian said. "I like hearing this. These are good tears."

"I didn't know he was bipolar," Nell said. "He never told me."

"Oh," Lillian said. "I assumed you knew."

"You'd think I'd figure it out if my boyfriend was bipolar."

"He took his meds. Until a month before he died."

"You knew that?" Nell asked.

"I found out from his psychiatrist. He told the psychiatrist that he was happy. That he didn't need medication anymore."

"He said that? That he was happy?"

"Yes. He was very happy," Lillian said. "You were good for him."

"I was?"

"He called you 'my girl,'" Lillian said. "My girl and I are going camping this weekend. My girl and I are auditioning for the same film. I thought it was very sweet."

"He was very sweet."

They were both quiet for a moment. Nell watched a small sailboat capsize as it tried to make its way to the pier. She could hear shrieks of laughter carry in the wind.

"So he went off his meds," Nell said.

"Then he told his psychiatrist that he didn't like himself

anymore. That he didn't like being inside his own head. The doctor begged him to go back on the medication."

"Why didn't he tell me?"

"He hated his condition. He didn't want it to rule his life."

"I wish I had known," Nell said.

There was a short pause, and then Lillian cleared her throat. "Would you like to come to lunch one day?"

"Yes," Nell said quickly. "I'd love that."

"I'd like that, too," Lillian said. "You can tell me stories about Chaney."

"He was wonderful. He was amazing."

"Thank you, Nell."

"Can I tell you one story? Now?"

"Of course," she said.

"Chaney told me that when he was eleven or so he was poking around in your room. It was right after his Dad died—I think he was looking for stuff that would remind him of his Dad. But he found your journal."

"Oh my."

Nell laughed. "Don't worry. He only read a couple of pages."

"Still," Lillian said. "I was a grieving widow. That wasn't something he should have ever seen."

"He told me that he learned that you were a woman. Not just a mom. And that it made him look at all women differently."

Lillian made a noise and Nell stopped talking.

"I shouldn't be telling you this," she said after a silence.

"No, please," Lillian said in a quiet voice. "Tell me more."

"He said that you wrote something about love being bigger

than anything else in the world. So big that sometimes you felt as if you'd burst at the seams. He didn't understand that. He was a kid. I think he was scared that you'd explode one day."

Lillian laughed. Nell smiled.

"And then one day, years later, he said he finally understood what you meant."

"Because he met you," Lillian said.

Nell began to cry. "I feel like I lost part of myself," she said. "I don't feel like I'm all here anymore."

"I know what you mean."

They were quiet again. Nell thought about last week's audition. She hadn't prepared. She wasn't in character. She needed Chaney to help her. On the way home from the audition she thought about the stories she'd tell Chaney. He'd want to hear about the director's black suit and red shoes. He'd love to watch her imitation of the guy who hammed all his lines and cried mid-monologue. By the time she got back to her house, she was almost surprised that Chaney wasn't there, that she lived someplace different, that she had no one to tell the stories.

"I'm in France right now," Nell said. "I'll be home next week. I'll give you another call then."

"France! What are you doing there?" Lillian asked.

"My mother's getting married."

"How wonderful."

Nell thought of saying: I invited a stranger I met on the plane and he ditched me this morning. My sister has gone AWOL. And I'm sitting on a rock drinking a beer.

Instead, she nodded. "Thanks for talking to me."

"Please," Lillian said. "You made me very happy today. Thank *you*, dear."

Chapter Eighteen

Gavin led Carly through the gritty streets of Marseille, his arm around her back, pressing her hip into his own. They were the same size, she noticed. Why had she thought he was taller?

He whispered in her ear, "I want to taste you on my lips."

Spare me, she thought. Damn her critical mind. Here she was, off on an adventure, and all she could do was snicker at the guy's come-on. Didn't she feel any stirring of lust or desire? She breathed him in. Stale wine. Had he been drinking this morning?

Just last night she had watched him across the table with Nell. She had imagined him naked, his penis impossibly big. Was she in the fantasy or her sister? Neither. Something about him made her think of sex, and yet nothing about him stirred her. She didn't want to fuck him.

She wanted to want him.

Did she ever lose herself to lust? She ran through the short list of boyfriends in her mind. The one guy in high school. Two in college. One in business school. Wesley. They were all good-looking, smart, ambitious. Not the point, she argued with herself. Did any of them make you wild with desire?

No.

Maybe she didn't know what desire was. Had she ever met a guy and pulsed with the need to seduce him? Her brain got in the way. Her body got pushed to the back of the line—think first, feel later. By the time she got to the physical response, her mind had already ticked off too many reasons not to go to bed with a guy.

And then when she did go to bed with him, she did what she was supposed to do. Foreplay, check. Blow job, check. Intercourse, check. Orgasm, check.

Did she ever lose herself in bed? Ha. She couldn't even imagine what it would mean to be lost. Carly always knew where Carly was.

No wonder she listened to the sounds of her sister's love-making last night with so much envy.

Nell knew lust. Nell's life was driven by physical desire, by animal passion. She fell for a guy and pounced. She did hot sweaty yoga and wrapped her arms around the other yogis at the end of class. Carly had seen her feast on a whole blueberry pie until her mouth was purple, her smile enormous. She swam naked in Lake Tahoe, she slept outside in the desert at night while the rest of the family climbed into tents. She danced at a nightclub, jacked up on Ecstasy, until the sun rose.

And now, here Carly was, having run off with the object of Nell's lust, and she could barely feel a thing.

Could she fake it? If she pretended to feel passion, would passion follow?

"Why do you lie?" Carly asked Gavin as they turned down a side street. Or was it an alleyway? The walls of the buildings were covered with graffiti, screaming graffiti in loud colors. Carly felt claustrophobic—not enough air, too much color.

"It's a game," Gavin said. "I like to play with people."

"Why?"

"I always win," he said.

"Were you playing a game with my sister?"

He led her down the center of the street, glancing from side to side, looking for something. Why was he walking so fast?

"Yes. She loved the game."

"And when you go back to the inn? What will you tell her?"

"I'm not going back."

Carly stopped walking. Gavin spun around to face her. There was no one else on the street, but she could hear loud music—the angry scream of a man and the wail of a guitar.

"Does Nell know?"

"By now she does," he said.

He stared at her, daring her. To do what? To keep walking? His eyes looked watery, unfocused. Was he high? Why did she think he was sexy last night? Now he looked like a con man, a used-car salesman, a hustler.

She thought of Nell, waking up to an empty bed this morning.

"I'm leaving," Carly said.

"You said you want to kiss me," he said, his voice low in his throat. "You want a good time."

She shook her head. His shirt was unbuttoned. She saw a tattoo on his chest—a black bomb, red flames sparking from the fuse. He's about to explode, she thought.

"Take me back to the inn," she said.

"That's not going to happen," he told her. His mouth edged into a crooked smile.

A door opened near them. Two teenage boys emerged, both skinny and jangly. Run, she thought.

"I'm leaving," she told Gavin, keeping her voice calm. "I'll get a cab back."

"You're coming with me," he said, reaching for her arm.

She pulled it away.

"Don't tell me what I'm doing," she said, anger rising inside her. She could feel a flush of heat, a surge of energy.

He grabbed her and pressed his mouth on hers. He pinned her arms to her sides and grinded against her with his pelvis. She could feel his erection, the gnash of his teeth on hers, the crush of his hands around her upper arms. She pushed one knee up, aiming for his crotch, hitting lower. He let go for a second and she turned to run.

"You want it!" he yelled. "You know you want it."

Above them a window slammed shut.

She ran for a long time, his words in her ear.

She reached the port somehow. The city streets dropped her there. On the side of a bus stop, Angelina Jolie smiled down at her. The poster was six feet tall. Angelina posed with a machine gun, wearing black lace-up boots and a corset that revealed bulging breasts. Carly stood and stared at it, uncomprehending. Beauty, she thought. Violence.

She kept walking.

She wanted to call her mother. She wanted to be young enough that her mother would swoop in and save her. But she was twenty-six and she had run off with her sister's boyfriend. She had blown off an outing that her mother's fiancé had planned. She couldn't call anyone.

She sat on a bench looking out at crowds of people milling past. She heard Spanish, French, German, and Japanese. An American mother, obese and sunburnt, snarled at her teenage son, "You try that again and I'll ground you for life." Carly pressed her fingers into her eyes.

She remembered yesterday, sitting at a café on the waterfront in Cassis. The waiter told Sébastien that she was sexy. Sébastien told her she would rule the world. She sipped champagne and watched the kayaks glide by.

Now, a dog came by, a mongrel, a beast with matted fur and pointy ears. He sniffed her legs.

"Go away," she said, her voice a surprise in her ears. She had forgotten that she had a voice.

The dog kept sniffing.

The wind stopped. She had been listening to its roar for so long and suddenly it was gone. On the horizon she saw black clouds.

She thought of Nell. She remembered a night, years ago, sitting in Nell's car at the side of the road, the policewoman waving a flashlight in her face. Nell stepped out of the car and the policewoman went away. She was wrecked, destroyed. Nell told her what to do, what to say, how to act.

Nell, she thought. I need you.

She pulled her phone out of her pocket and turned it on. She had missed dozens of calls—her mother, Nell, Wes, her mother, Wes, her mother again and again. Her mother's wedding weekend. Olivia's joy, spreading across the dinner table, wrapping its arms around everyone but her.

You know you want it.

What do I want?

Nell. I want Nell.

She clicked on Nell's name and held her breath while the phone began to ring.

Chapter Nineteen

Olivia looked out the window of her room at the inn. Brody and his mother stood near the arbor, deep in conversation. Olivia could see the back of Brody's head, tilted to one side, his hand reaching out to his mother.

Fanny slapped his hand away.

Brody's arm dropped to his side. Olivia couldn't see his expression. But Fanny's face was twisted in anger. She shook her head, turning away from Brody, her arms crossed against her chest.

Brody stepped closer and his mother shouted something— Olivia couldn't hear the words but her window seemed to rattle with the force of Fanny's anger.

A moment later, Fanny turned and stormed off, her body quivering with rage.

Brody dropped into a chair under the arbor.

Olivia could barely see him; wisteria draped down from the wooden trellis and obscured her view of the table.

She pushed open the window.

"Brody," she called.

He leaned back in his chair and looked up at her.

He shook his head. "Did not go as planned."

"Come up?" Olivia asked.

"Let's get out of here," Brody said. "Meet me at the gate."

"Where we going?"

"Beats the hell out of me," he said.

They left the inn and walked toward town, their arms intertwined. The day was hot and still; without the wind, a welcome quiet descended on the valley. They passed a field of artichokes and a farmhouse with white sheets drying on the clothesline. Children's voices rang out over the high wall of a villa.

"So what happened?" Olivia asked.

Brody shrugged. "She says it serves him right. Let him die alone in his goddamn cabin by the creek."

"What?"

"He left her. He hurt her. She doesn't want him back."

"That's impossible."

"I've never seen my mother that angry."

Olivia stopped walking and pulled Brody toward her.

"I get this," she said.

"What?"

"I'm not big on pain. When something hurts a little too much I turn it into anger."

"I've never seen you do that."

"I'm saving it for after you marry me," Olivia said with a smile.

"You devil," Brody said, stroking her chin with the back of his hand.

"She can't stand to lose Sam. She can't even begin to feel that pain. So she's pushing him away. It's easier."

"Do all women do this?"

"Only the best women," Olivia said.

Brody shook his head. "So what happens next?"

"It might take her some time. She'll be angry for a little while."

"And then?"

"Maybe she'll take him back."

"They're both crazy," Brody said, running his hand through his hair. "One flees and then the other flees."

"If I thought I was going to lose you I'd be a crazy woman."

"You're not going to lose me."

"Ever?"

Brody leaned forward to kiss her.

A car honked. They looked toward the street; a Peugeot pulled to a stop beside them. Emily rolled down the window.

"Are you guys making out on the street?" she asked. "We have rooms at the inn for that."

Olivia blew her a kiss.

"Go visit that winery," Emily told them. She pointed to the gate at the side of the road. "Tell Monsieur LeBlanc that I sent you."

"Is that an order?"

"It is. And then crawl back to the inn. I promise you lots of privacy in Room 5."

"*Oui, madame,*" Olivia said.

Emily sped off.

"*Un verre de vin, mademoiselle?*" Brody asked.

"*Bien sûr,*" Olivia said, and they turned into the winery.

After failing to understand the garbled voice through the intercom, Olivia pushed the gate, holding it open for Brody.

"My French sucks," she said.

"So does mine," Brody told her. "But we're really good at wine tasting."

Hand in hand, they walked up the long driveway to a large apricot-colored villa at the top of the hill. They were surrounded by vineyards, long rows of grapevines hugging the land.

An elderly man greeted them at the door.

"*Bonjour! Entrez! Vous êtes venus pour une dégustation?*"

"*Oui,*" Olivia said, relieved that she could understand him. He spoke slowly, probably accustomed to tourists. "*Je suis une amie de Emily Bourdon.*"

"Ah, Emily!" the man said. And then he recited the charms of Olivia's best friend at great length.

As he spoke he led them around the villa to a terra-cotta patio behind the house. He offered them seats at a small wrought-iron table. And then he disappeared.

Here the grapevines stretched for a very long distance and seemed to tumble into the sea. Olivia felt as if she were looking at a painting divided in three parts: vineyard, sea, sky, each one its own rich color. Far in the distance the first clouds hovered.

Two glasses of white wine appeared on the table in front of them.

"*Merci,*" Olivia said.

"C'est magnifique," Brody said, gesturing at the view.

"Mais, oui," the man said, bowing. He described the wine in language that was lost to Olivia though she kept nodding in appreciation. *"Et, voilà,"* he finally said, and gestured for them to sip. He, too, held a glass. He brought it to his lips as if tasting the wine for the very first time.

"C'est bon," he announced and again, he disappeared.

"C'est délicieux," Olivia said.

"Imagine this," Brody. "We live here. We end every day right here with a glass of wine and a view of our paradise."

Olivia shook her head. "That's not what I want," she said.

Brody looked at her, surprised.

"I want the mess of our lives," she said. "I want San Francisco and my crazy daughters and Wyoming and your crazy parents. I want it all, not just the pretty stuff."

"Olivia, your girls are grown up. My parents are responsible for themselves. This is all about us now. Our lives. Our future."

"You're right," Olivia said. "But I'm never going to be done as a parent. Your own mother said that. And I don't want to be done. They're going to get married and have kids and then our lives get even more complicated. I want the whole damn mess."

Brody sipped his wine, staring out toward the sea.

"Why didn't you have kids?" Olivia asked, her voice quiet.

"Grace didn't want them," Brody said. He squinted as if looking for something on the horizon.

"You never told me that."

He shrugged. "She felt like the world was too dangerous a place. She had grown up in New York and when she was twenty a couple of teenage boys stole her purse and beat her up pretty badly. She fled the city and escaped to Wyoming. When we met she told me right away that she didn't feel strong enough to have children. I don't mean physically. She was strong enough to raise a barn. But she didn't want to worry about the fragility of children. How hard it was to protect them from danger."

"What did you want?" Olivia asked.

"I wanted her. And so I gave up on the idea of kids."

Olivia sipped her wine. She heard a grumble of thunder in the distance. The clouds were far away; it seemed as if a storm was something that couldn't happen in this valley, with all this blinding sun.

"We'll learn how to do this," she said, reaching for Brody's hand.

When they got back to the inn, Brody headed up to their room while Olivia walked into the kitchen for a bottle of water and a couple of glasses. On her way up the stairs she heard loud voices coming from one of the rooms.

She tiptoed down the hall. A door opened just as she reached it. Emily almost toppled into her.

"Sorry—"

"Excuse me—"

Olivia glanced in the open door. Jake lay in bed, the sheets twisted around him, his hair a tousled mess. His chest was bare. The room smelled dank.

"It's not what you think," Emily said.

Olivia stared at her. "What is it?"

"Nothing."

Emily reached for the door and slammed it closed.

"It doesn't look like nothing," Olivia said.

"I wanted—I don't know what I wanted," Emily muttered. Her eyes were red and swollen.

"Revenge sex?" Olivia asked.

"Just one time."

"You thought that would even things up?"

"I don't know what I thought," Emily said, her face pale.

"Did it? Are you done now?" Olivia asked, her voice loud.

"Jake kicked me out before I climbed into his bed," Emily said. She turned and marched down the hallway. "God damn him."

Olivia could hear her heavy steps on the stairs.

Chapter Twenty

Nell was swimming laps in the pool when she heard her cellphone ringing. She pulled herself out of the water and grabbed
the phone off the lounge chair.

"Carly," she said, a wave of relief washing over her.

"I'm sorry," Carly said. "I know you called."

"Mom's been crazy worried. Where the hell are you?"

"I need a ride," Carly said. "I'm in Marseille. Can you
come get me?"

"What? What are you doing in Marseille?" Nell asked, but
then she realized: Gavin. Sébastien had told her that the car had
been found in Marseille. In the silence she began to imagine her
sister in bed with Gavin, their limbs intertwined, their bodies
slick with sweat. "Tell me about your sister," he had said. Fuck

Gavin. Fuck Carly. Which is just what they had been doing all day.

"I asked you a goddamn question," Nell said.

"Listen," Carly said, her voice wobbly. "I need help. I'm stuck here."

"Get a fucking taxi. I'm not your limo service," Nell said, and she hung up.

She dropped into the lounge chair, the phone in her hand. Her eyes started to well up. He wanted her, not me.

The phone buzzed in her hand.

"Did you think I wouldn't figure it out?" Nell spat into the phone.

"Please," Carly said. "I need help."

"You need help? You steal my guy and you fucking need help?"

Nell could hear the pulse of her heart. She felt panicky, as if she might scream or sob or flee.

"Nothing happened," Carly said, her voice so quiet that Nell had to strain to hear her. "I was walking to town—"

"Spare me the details."

"I need you," Carly said in a voice Nell had never heard before. "I need your help. Please."

"You can call a cab," Nell said, though the anger was gone from her voice.

"Please, Nell. I can't come back right now. I just want to be with you."

Nell stood up and looked around. Everyone except for Sébastien was gone—she had no idea where they all were. When she had walked back from town she had expected to find them still at the table, enjoying a marathon meal like last night's dinner. But the kitchen was clean, the doors to all the bedrooms were closed and the pool beckoned her.

"Where are you?" she muttered into the phone.

"At the Vieux Port," Carly said. Nell could hear the relief in her voice.

"You always get what you want," Nell said. "No matter what you do. You always win."

"I'm not winning anything," Carly whispered.

"I'll call you when I get there," Nell said, hanging up the phone.

Nell walked through the open door of the inn and found Sébastien sitting at the front desk. He was staring at the computer and didn't look away until she stopped in front of him.

"Can I borrow your car?" she asked.

"Emily has the car. She went to the market. I have the motorcycle."

"I'll take it."

"Where are you going?"

"Marseille."

"You cannot go after Gavin," Sébastien said. *"C'est fou."*

Nell rolled her eyes. "It's Carly. Somehow she ended up there." Why was she covering for her sister? Why not tell the world: Carly ran off with my guy!

"Carly?" Sébastien said. "Why is she in Marseille?"

"Who knows," Nell said.

Sébastien reached into a drawer and pulled out a set of keys. "You can ride a motorcycle?"

"I once rode a Ducati from Santa Monica to Big Sur and back in a day."

He tossed them to Nell. "Do not get into trouble," he said.

Trouble, she thought. It's not me. It's my sister.

When the cops arrested Nell for the pills they found in her pocket after the high school dance, she felt an odd sense of calm. I can handle this, she thought.

"Let me drop off my sister first," she told the police officers.

"Call someone to pick her up," the male cop said.

Nell had pulled out her cellphone and called her mom. She told her to come immediately, that she was being taken in to the police station for questioning, that Carly was sick and needed to go to bed. When Olivia flipped out, Nell calmly said, "Just get here, Mom. No drama right now, okay?" and then gave her the address.

Nell felt suddenly grown-up. No one was telling her what to do. She was making important decisions, decisions that would affect her in all kinds of ways. It felt both terrifying and absolutely right.

"Let me go wait with my sister," she told the cops, and they nodded.

Nell climbed into the front seat of her car.

"Stop crying," she told her sister. "You have to listen to me."

"I'm so scared," Carly said, her voice quiet.

"You're going to be fine. But you have to do what I tell you. They're going to arrest me now. Mom is coming to get you. Tell her that you have some kind of bug. The flu. Anything. You can cry, you can throw up, but remember that you're sick. You're done being high. You feel lousy and you want to climb in bed. Do you get that?"

Carly nodded.

"No one at school can know about you taking drugs. Do you get that?"

"Why are they arresting you?" Carly asked. "Were you speeding?"

"I rolled a stop sign."

"They don't arrest people for that."

"I know," Nell said, thinking about jail for the first time.

"Call Dad," Carly said.

"Yeah. Good idea," Nell said. "Where is he?" He had left on a business trip earlier that week.

"New York, I think," Carly said.

Nell pulled out her phone. Her father picked up on the first ring.

"Dad," she said. "I need your help."

"I was sound asleep."

"I just got arrested."

"What?"

"They're arresting me for possession."

Carly shot Nell a terrified look; Nell waved her hand through the air as if all these problems would fly away.

"Of what?" her dad asked.

"Just get someone to meet me at the station. Okay?"

"How did they find it?"

"They took my jacket," Nell said. "And they found a pill bottle in my pocket."

"Illegal search," he said. "I'll send someone right away."

Nell felt comfortable on Sébastien's motorcycle within minutes. I need a bike, she thought, climbing out of Cassis on a
winding mountain road. She remembered telling her mother
that she was going to buy a bike a few years ago, after riding
her friend's Ducati for the weekend. Olivia went ballistic,
threatening to cut off her money. Here she was, twenty-eight,
still taking money from her mom. Her dad had cut her off
when she was busted at eighteen, telling her it was tough love.
Grow up. Get a job. Olivia gave her money on the sly for
years, and then after the divorce she set up an account for Nell,
sending her $500 every month.

She was kicked out of school after the arrest, even though
her father got them to drop the charges because of the illegal
search. UC Santa Cruz first rescinded its offer of acceptance
and later, once the charges were dropped, agreed to let her attend if she finished her last semester of high school. But Nell
said no, that she had other plans. In fact, she felt untethered to
any life plan.

She never told anyone—except for Chaney, years later—
that the drugs belonged to her sister. Weeks after Nell's arrest,
Carly began her prestigious Google internship. Did Carly
know that Nell saved her ass? Nell wasn't sure. They never
talked about it. Carly might have been too fucked-up that night
to remember what happened. But Nell was sure that she had
made the right decision. Carly was destined for so much success; a drug bust could have jeopardized everything. Nell was
destined for jack shit. After the bust, she left town, drove to
L.A., found a room in a house with a bunch of struggling actors and drifted. Ten years later and she was still drifting.

Would it have been different if she had finished high school and gone to college? Maybe. But she could have done that at any time along the way.

She sped along the road to Marseille, hugging the mountain along the coast. She leaned into the curves, feeling bolder and stronger with each turn. When she entered the city she pulled over and opened the map on her iPhone. There it was: VIEUX PORT. She tucked the phone back into her pocket and headed seaward.

The port was bigger than she had imagined, a sprawling area that had been cleaned up for the tourists. Around the busy harbor were shops, restaurants, office buildings, even a market on the promenade. She parked the bike and called Carly.

"Where are you?" she asked, her voice still tinged with anger.

"Are you at the port?" Carly asked.

"Yes. I'm looking at some weird sculpture thing. It's a mirrored ceiling or something. In the middle of the promenade."

"I'll meet you there in five minutes," Carly said. "I'm right down the street."

It wasn't long before Nell saw Carly approaching from the other end of the harbor. She walked with her head down, her shoulders slumped. Not Carly's usual jaunty walk.

Carly led them toward a bench at the edge of the port, overlooking the harbor. They sat with a wide space between them.

"I just got a ride from him," Carly said, her voice soft.

"You're full of shit."

They sat in silence for a while. Nell watched two very tanned guys fixing the mast of a sailboat. They were muscular but wiry, both with bleached-blond hair that curled over their ears. Brothers, she thought. Is that easier? She couldn't imagine working side by side with Carly. Why was it so hard to do right by her?

"Talk to me," Nell finally said.

Chapter Twenty-one

Carly felt as if she hadn't slept in days, weeks. She remembered the crush of work before she left for France. EyeDate was gearing up for an international launch so she had spent hours interviewing managers for new offices. She'd been overwhelmed by the paperwork to incorporate in each country; the Brazilian consulate had been particularly troublesome. On top of all that, they were at the tail end of another round of fundraising. Most of the high-level bullet points were sorted out but the lawyers were still arguing about the fine print.

Now she couldn't imagine returning to work and diving back into all of that unfinished business. She wanted to do nothing. She had never done nothing.

"What do you do all day?" she asked Nell, who sat beside her on the bench.

"What?" Nell asked. "What are you talking about?"

"Maybe I'll quit work. Take time off."

"You can't quit work, Carly. Not when the company's about to go public."

"Just tell me what you do all day."

"You're trying to figure out the life of a bum? It's really hard, Carly. You have to sleep as late as you can. You switch clothes from your pajamas to your yoga clothes, which are just like pajamas only tighter. You go to yoga class. You go to a café. You memorize your four lines for your thirty seconds in that week's episode of "Crappy Cop Show." You go to a bar because it's five o'clock. Some guy buys you a drink. The night disappears. You wake up the next morning and hope this one's different."

Sounds wonderful, Carly thought. Sounds dreamy. No meetings, no deadlines, no reports. No Wes lying in bed next to you, his iPad on his lap.

"I didn't sleep with Gavin," she said.

"Why don't you tell me what you did do?" Nell said.

"I got in his car," Carly said. She heard thunder, like the low growl of an angry dog. The sky was still blue, the air suddenly still. The wind had been howling in her ear all day. And now it had stopped. Something hovered in the air, the echo of all that absent noise.

"That's a start," Nell said.

"He wanted to go to Marseille," Carly said. "I wanted an adventure. I wanted to step outside of my life. I wanted to be you."

"You have never wanted to be me for one second in your life," Nell said.

"I don't know what passion is," Carly said, looking at Nell.

Nell waited a moment, considering this. "You have passion for your job," she offered.

"Maybe once. Now it's just a job."

"Wes?"

Carly shook her head. "He's a great big mind. An enormous mind. His penis is hiding behind an iPad."

Nell burst out laughing. Carly finally smiled.

"Don't be mad at me," she said and reached out her hand.

Nell crossed her arms over her chest. Carly's hand drifted in the air for a moment and then dropped.

"You took off with my guy," Nell said flatly.

"I did. I'm sorry," Carly said. "I kissed him and didn't feel a thing."

"I'm supposed to feel good about that? You run off with my guy and then you don't find him hot enough for you? Are you fucking nuts, Carly?"

"Yes," she said, her voice quiet.

"I don't know what's going on here," Nell said. She stood up, shaking her head.

Carly saw two guys on a sailboat eyeing Nell. They didn't even look at Carly. I don't exist, she thought. I've disappeared into thin air.

"Bonjour!" one of the guys called out. *"Tu veux une bière, chérie?"*

Nell walked toward their boat. She didn't hesitate. Cute guys, a sexy sailboat, a cold beer. She didn't look back at Carly. Who needs a confused sister when you can have all that testosterone in such close quarters? Sure enough, Nell hopped onboard the boat. She offered her cheeks, first one and then the other, as if she were French, as if she knew these men, as if she did this every day of her life. Carly didn't even know which cheek to kiss first. How could she have taught herself programming, yet she doesn't know how to kiss French-style?

Nell chatted with the guys for a moment, accepted a beer and a seat. They both faced her, their hunger for her as apparent as her own delight in them.

How do you do that? Carly thought. I would have said no. I would have considered the danger of unknown men and unfamiliar territory. But Nell sat there in the hot sun, already laughing, the men leaning forward as if drawn to the bright shining light of her.

Nell never looked back at her sister.

One of the guys got up, grabbed a baseball cap hanging from the wheel of the boat and put it on Nell's head. She stood up and spun around, modeling the hat. The man put his hand on Nell's ass and Nell smacked it away. The men roared with laughter.

Get away from there, Carly thought.

But one of the men headed down the steps of the boat to the galley below and Nell followed.

Carly stood up and cleared her throat. Don't go down there, she thought.

The other man followed Nell.

Go get her. Get her out of there, Carly told herself. But she stood there and the sky flashed with lightning. Carly blinked. Nell was gone. The three of them, down in the belly of the boat.

You don't know them, Nell.

Carly took a few steps toward the boat. Thunder rolled in

the distance, a long foghorn of sound. And then the world fell oddly silent, as if waiting for what would come next.

Let her go, she thought. Nell takes care of herself. But there are two men. Strangers. No one to hear her cries for help.

She walked along the dock until she reached the side of the boat. She could hear voices; she could smell marijuana.

When she stepped onto the boat, it rocked and she grabbed the guardrail for support.

"*Qui est là?*" a man's voice called out. He sounded angry.

Run, she thought, but instead she took a few hesitant steps toward the back of the boat and almost barreled into one of the men, who was leaping up the stairs from the galley.

"*Et oui? Excusez-moi?*"

"*Ma sœur,*" Carly said tentatively. Was that the word? My sister?

"Carly?" Nell called, and her face appeared in the opening of the galley.

"I thought maybe you were in trouble," Carly said quickly, under her breath.

"You think you're my fucking savior?" Nell asked. "Is that it? After all these years you think you owe me one?"

Again, lightning flashed, this time followed by a loud crack of thunder.

"Holy shit," Nell said, her face quickly changing as she remembered. "I've got the bike."

The other man appeared behind Nell, joint in hand, smile on his face. "*Tu veux?*" he asked, offering the joint to Carly. She shook her head.

"We've got to beat the rain," Nell said. "*On y va.*"

She turned and kissed the guy behind her, then the other

guy. It was hard to tell them apart. Twins? Both looked extraordinarily stoned and pleased.

"*Ciao, mes amis,* " Nell said.

She jumped off the boat. Carly turned and followed sheepishly.

I want to go home, she thought. But where's home? Her house with Wes in Palo Alto? Her mother's house in San Francisco? Then she thought about the inn, Emily's beautiful inn, and she ached to be in her single room at the top of the stairs.

She raced to keep up with her sister.

"Nell!" Carly called.

Nell looked back, her mouth twisted in disgust. "Hurry," she said. She was still wearing the baseball cap the guys had given her. It was bleached to a pale lemon color and marked with sweat stains. I would toss it in the garbage, Carly thought. But Nell wore it proudly, her wide eyes vibrant below the visor.

"I'm sorry," Carly said, catching up to her and fast-walking at her side.

"Yeah, I heard you," Nell told her. "Call Mom. Let her know that you're okay."

"I don't know what to tell her," Carly said.

She thought of her parents' bedroom in the house they lived in when she was a child. She would wake up in the middle of the night and climb into bed next to her mother, taking a part of her mom's flannel nightgown and pressing it up against her nose. Then she would sleep like that, holding on.

"You went for a walk on the beach. You lay down on some rocks and fell asleep for a few hours."

"That's ridiculous," Carly said.

"So tell the truth," Nell said. "Whatever the hell that is."

Carly looked down at her feet, racing across the pavement.

Nell pulled out her phone and tapped on it. "I've got Carly," she said after a moment.

Carly could hear the buzz of her mother's voice, a rush of words that came spilling out. She remembered waking up one night when she was a child to the sound of a glass breaking. She heard laughter and lots of people talking at once. She padded downstairs in her pajamas and found her mother on the couch in the living room, surrounded by so many people and so much noise that the room felt as if it were shaking. A party, her mother told her. We're having a party. Carly climbed onto her mother's lap and watched the party for the rest of the night right there, tucked in her mother's arms.

"I'm bringing her back. We'll be there soon."

Carly wrapped her arms tightly around her sister's waist. She had never been on a motorcycle. When Nell revved the engine and took off, Carly felt dizzy with fear. And then she rested her head on her sister's back and disappeared. It didn't matter if the road seemed to rise up and move away, if the noise pounded her head, if the sky lit up with lightning or rocked with thunder. She had her arms around her sister, her face pressed into her back.

And then, finally, they were turning into the driveway of the inn. She looked up. Olivia and Brody stood at the top of the driveway waiting for them.

She climbed off the bike. She turned around and already her mother was at her side and then she was in her arms and Carly held on to her as if something might sweep her away.

Part Three

Chapter Twenty-two

The mistral came through during the night, pummeling the earth with rain. The wind howled through the trees, knocking down branches. Olivia watched from the bedroom window and saw a large patio umbrella crash into the swimming pool. The inn creaked and groaned while the storm raged.

Her daughter was back. But something was wrong. In the middle of the night, standing alone by the window, Olivia was sure that something had happened to Carly. She didn't believe her daughter had fallen asleep on the beach. Some other story was etched into Carly's face.

She climbed back into bed and finally fell asleep, the noise of the storm penetrating her dreams.

When she woke up, hours later, Olivia wrapped her arms around Brody's back. He was still sleeping, still warm and bear-like. Olivia buried her nose in his neck. He smelled of the woods, of the earth. She loved his smell.

"Are you trying to seduce me on my wedding day?" he murmured.

"Yes," she said. "I want you to have one last romp as a single man."

He turned toward her and took her in his arms. "It's still raining," he said.

"It will stop," she said. "It's our wedding day."

The rain pelted against the windows and the wind whistled. Brody kissed her neck, her chest, her breasts. She closed her eyes and breathed him in. Safe, she thought. He makes me feel safe.

But it's an illusion. No one's safe. Her daughter disappeared for a day and came back changed somehow.

"Be with me," Brody murmured in her ear.

"I'm right here," she said. "I'm with you."

He always knew when she was lost in her thoughts. When they made love, he demanded all of her, her attention, her physical being, her presence. She looked at him and smiled.

"I'm going to marry you today," she said.

"Damn right," he said, kissing her.

And then she pushed her thoughts away and let herself fall into him. Take me away. She lost herself as his hands moved over her body. Sex with Brody was still new, even after a year of thrilling each other in bed. Now she found herself wanting him with a kind of urgency that surprised her. Take me with you. When he buried his head between her legs she let herself fly. And when he entered her and made love to her slowly, holding her gaze in his, she felt herself land again. With him. Her new home.

When they were done they lay in each other's arms.

"Marriage isn't going to change that, is it?" Olivia asked.

"Not a chance," Brody said.

"You won't become bored?"

"With this body? Not possible."

"This body is getting old."

"So is this one," he said, patting his slight paunch. "We're going to do that together."

They were quiet for a while, holding each other. Olivia started to feel herself drift off—she had been awake for too long in the middle of the night. Brody pulled her closer to him. Hang on, she thought. Keep me safe.

And then her eyes opened and she knew what had happened.

"She was with Gavin," Olivia said.

"What? Who?" Brody peered at her.

"Carly. She spent the day with Gavin. Nell was furious with her—did you notice?"

"She fell asleep on the beach," Brody said.

Olivia sat up in bed. "No. They were lying."

"Why would they lie?"

"I don't know," she said, standing up. "But I know they're lying."

Brody pushed himself up in bed. "Where are you going? Come back to bed. Talk to me."

Olivia sat down on the side of the bed and looked at him. He reached for her hand.

"I was up for a long time in the middle of the night," she said quietly.

"You should have woken me."

"You can't make all my worries go away."

"Why not?"

She leaned over and kissed him. "I wouldn't mind making all your problems go away either. It just doesn't work that way."

"What problems? I don't have any problems."

Olivia shook her head. "I'm taking a shower. And then I'm going to check in on Carly."

"First tell me what we have to do this morning," Brody said. "To get ready."

"We're ready," she told him. "We are so ready."

Olivia stood outside of Carly's door. She couldn't hear any movement inside. She knew Carly needed her rest, but now Olivia felt rattled. She wanted to know what happened yesterday.

She turned the doorknob and stopped for a moment when the door creaked. Then she pushed slowly and poked her head inside. She could see Carly in bed, her back to the door. The room was dark, the drapes pulled tight. Olivia wanted to move through the room, opening the windows, letting in light and air. She could smell something sour.

Carly was always a light sleeper, even as a child. But now she didn't stir. And Olivia couldn't make herself wake her. She pulled the door closed.

When she felt a hand on her shoulder, she flinched.

"Sorry," Emily whispered. "She's still sleeping?"

"Yes," Olivia said. "Come have coffee with me."

"Good idea," Emily said.

"Promise me you didn't just come out of Jake's room."

Emily rolled her eyes. "It was a mistake. It was a crazy idea."

"Who knew the guy would save you from yourself?"

"Jerk," Emily muttered.

Olivia laughed.

"But it did help me figure something out," Emily said. "I don't really want to have sex with someone else. Even now."

"Good," Olivia said.

Emily linked arms with her, and they walked downstairs and into the kitchen.

"Where is everyone?" Olivia asked.

"Fanny went for a walk in the rain. Jake's still sleeping, I think. Sébastien's cleaning up some storm damage," Emily said. "And Nell's working on a surprise for you."

"Really?"

"It's very nice."

"How unlike Nell," she said.

"Cut your daughter some slack, O."

Olivia stood up. "Hey. That's not fair."

"You're a little too tough on her."

"She needs a little tough in her life."

"She did a good job taking care of her sister yesterday," Emily said. "Sit down. Here's your coffee."

Olivia did not sit down. She glared at Emily. "People who don't have kids think there are rules for how to do this. There are no rules. Each kid is so different that you have to figure out what's right for each one. What Nell needs is very different from what Carly needs. Always has been."

"Thanks for the parenting lecture," Emily said, passing her an espresso.

Olivia dropped onto her stool, all the fire gone from inside of her. "Sorry, Em," she said. "I didn't sleep well."

"She's back. Everything's fine."

"I'm not sure."

"What do you mean?" Emily sat next to Olivia. They both looked out at the garden. The rain fell steadily. One of the chairs had toppled over and the umbrella was perched on its side.

"Doesn't exactly look like a wedding day, does it?" Olivia said, warming her hands on the cup.

"We'll have the wedding inside," Emily assured her. "It will be perfect."

"What happened last night?" Olivia asked. "After dinner."

The guests had eaten a light dinner poolside. Paolo had prepared a pasta puttanesca and a salad, both delicious. But Carly had gone right to her room, assuring Olivia that she wasn't hungry. She just needed to sleep and she'd be fine tomorrow.

After dinner Olivia and Brody had excused themselves and headed to their own room. "We need our beauty rest," they had explained.

"Nell and Jake played *boules* against Fanny and Sébastien," Emily said. "Jake and Sébastien drank too much. I was almost glad when it started raining. I think Jake went into town. Everyone else went to their rooms."

"How are you and Sébastien doing?"

"I don't know," Emily said. "I'm still ignoring him. We'll deal with our marriage after we've gotten you two hitched."

"You could forgive him," Olivia said.

"You want my lecture?" she said with a wry smile. "Unmarried people think they know so much about marriage. They have no idea that each marriage is different and there are no damn rules on how to make it work."

"Touché," Olivia said.

"The truth is that I love him and I'm in a rage. I keep imagining him in bed with that horrible woman. Naked. The body I know so well on top of that woman's body. That penis I know so well finding its way into that woman's body."

"It's awful. Push that image out of your head."

"I can't," Emily said. "Sex is the most intimate part of our lives. Sébastien and I sleep wrapped in each other's arms. Did he hold her like that? Did he stroke her breasts the way he touches mine?"

"Stop," Olivia said. "You're torturing yourself."

"No. He's torturing me. He did this to me."

"But if it didn't mean anything?"

"How can it not mean anything?" Emily said, her voice rising. "It's what we do when we're closest, when we're most connected. It's how we love each other without saying a word. You can do the same thing with someone else and it doesn't mean anything?"

"Maybe it's not the same thing," Olivia said meekly.

"Sex is sex is sex," Emily said. "You get naked, you take parts of yourself and merge them. You disappear into each other. My God, he used to tell me that we had better sex than he had ever had in his life."

"Is that still true?" Olivia asked.

"Don't turn this on me," Emily said. "I know that argument. A guy doesn't cheat unless he's not getting it at home. Unless his wife ignores him or denies him pleasure. Wrong. This is not my fault."

Olivia put her hand on Emily's. "I know that," she said, her voice soft.

Emily shook her head. "We don't have sex as often as we did in the old days," she said quietly. "We've been together a long time. And we're busy with the inn. I'm running from one task to the other all day. I'm exhausted at night."

"But you just said it: That doesn't excuse him. That doesn't mean he can go looking for it elsewhere."

"I don't know what it means," Emily said. "I want my marriage back. That's the stupid truth. I love him and I want him back." She stood up and walked to the window. "I hate the damn rain," she mumbled.

"Do you want a distraction?"

Emily turned and looked at her. "Anything. Get my mind off that woman's fat naked ass."

"I think Nell and Carly are lying about what happened yesterday. I think Carly might have gone off with Gavin."

"Carly and Gavin?"

"I don't know for sure."

"That's crazy. Carly wouldn't do that to her sister."

"Nell's not talking to Carly. She's not even looking at her."

"Go ask her."

"Nell?"

"I'll go get her," Emily said. "I don't want you to see what she's doing."

Emily left the kitchen and Olivia stared out the window at the sheet of rain. Her wedding day. No matter what.

Olivia walked into the parlor of the inn, a room that was used as a lounge for the guests. There were a couple of seating areas with tables for board games and jigsaw puzzles. There were also reading chairs and a long side table that was set up as a bar.

We can do the wedding here, she thought. We'll move the furniture and bring in flowers. We don't need chairs—the few guests can just gather around. It will be cozy and sweet. Not beautiful like Emily's garden, but that doesn't matter. It's about the ceremony and the guests.

"Mom," Nell said, startling her.

"What do you think of this room for the wedding?" Olivia asked.

"Sure. Why not?"

"We'll get all this furniture out of the way. It might work."

"Is that why you wanted me?" Nell asked. "To move furniture?"

"No," Olivia said. "Sit here with me."

She gestured to two reading chairs in front of the fireplace. Nell walked over and dropped into one; Olivia sat in the other.

"Thanks for getting your sister yesterday," Olivia said.

"Of course," Nell said quickly.

"I don't understand why Carly didn't call me."

Nell brushed her hair out of her eyes. She looked rumpled and unkempt. Olivia hoped she had brought something nice to wear to the wedding. Nell didn't have much fashion sense. She chose to live in her yoga clothes or jeans and a tank top. Did she own nice clothes? I should have taken her shopping, Olivia thought.

"Carly didn't want to bother you," Nell said. "She already felt so bad about missing the kayaking trip."

Olivia leaned forward. "Nell, I want you to tell me the truth."

Nell regathered herself in her chair, tucking her legs under her. She looked everywhere except at her mother.

"Sure," she finally said. "About what?"

"Yesterday."

Nell scrunched up her face. Olivia loved her daughter's impish beauty. Even as a kid, Nell was the master of faces, always showing so much emotion by the lift of an eyebrow, the purse of her lips. No wonder she chose acting. She could be a mime with that face alone.

"What are you talking about?" Nell asked. She leaned over and put her elbows on her knees, then perched her face in her hands. She opened her eyes wide.

"I have an odd feeling about it," Olivia said. "That she didn't wander the beaches and sleep on a rock. That something else happened and you girls aren't telling me."

Nell rolled her eyes. "That's ridiculous."

"Is it?"

Now Nell made an exasperated face. "You're a drama queen," she said.

"I was just thinking about your acting ability," Olivia said, smiling. "It's in every expression you make."

"Nothing else happened yesterday. She needs to sleep more. And she needs a better boyfriend."

"You sure?"

"Yeah, he's a bore."

"Are you sure nothing else happened?"

Olivia watched her daughter carefully. Nell picked a piece of lint off her yoga pants. But after a moment, she looked up and held her mother's stare.

"Nothing else happened."

She's still lying, Olivia thought. She's a good actress, but not that good.

"How are *you* doing?" Olivia asked.

"Me? I'm fine. I'm great."

"Wow. That's a good way to shut me up."

Nell smiled, a beautiful smile that lit up her face.

"I'm okay. Still missing Chaney. Still trying to figure out what the hell I'm doing with my life. But I'm getting closer."

Olivia nodded. "I love you, sweetheart."

"Yeah, I know. It's your specialty." And then she rolled her eyes again. "Listen, Mom," she said, jumping out of her seat as if she could no longer sit still. "Carly and I are going to do your hair and makeup. Before the wedding. We're meeting you in your room at noon. Brody will be banished. He's not allowed to see you until you walk down the aisle."

Olivia felt a jolt of pleasure. "Wow," she said. "Really?"

"Really. You're lousy with makeup. And you can't just wear your hair like you do every day. It's a fucking wedding."

"It's a fucking wedding," Olivia agreed, a smile spreading across her face.

Chapter Twenty-three

Nell had thought of the chuppah in the middle of the night. When the storm woke her, she climbed out of bed and stood at the window for a while, watching the rain pound the swimming pool. She felt sad for her mother that the wedding would have to be indoors—she knew how much Olivia wanted a garden wedding. Emily's garden. She thought of the weddings she had gone to over the years—cousins, friends. And in her imagination something made Olivia's indoor wedding suddenly beautiful: a chuppah.

Nell's parents were Jewish but they hadn't done much to raise the girls in the faith. A year or two at Sunday school until Nell got kicked out for playing hooky too many times. High Holiday services every so often until Olivia realized that she'd rather stay home and meditate. Nell's dad still went to temple once in a while—a reform temple in San Francisco—but she suspected that he was more concerned about business contacts than spiritual salvation. Nell felt ambivalent about being Jewish—she didn't like the religion but she did like the culture. Until she left for L.A., the family had Passover seders with their Marin cousins; it was all about the food, the wine, the good company.

She knew that a chuppah was some kind of covering that the bride and groom stood under during the service. She wasn't sure what it meant—she'd check on her iPhone or Sébastien's computer in the morning—but she liked the look of it, the sense of the couple being held by something. She needed to find a beautiful fabric and attach it at the four corners to sticks or poles. She imagined this: She, Carly, Fanny, and Emily could hold the four poles, creating a canopy over her mother and Brody for the wedding ceremony.

When she woke in the morning she found Emily and told her the plan. Emily loved it and suggested Nell head down to the Cassis farmers' market right away—surely she'd find some great fabric there. So Nell borrowed Emily's car, found the market at the edge of town, and wandered the stalls in the rain.

She bought croissants for everyone at one stand, *Camembert* at another, a floppy summer hat for herself at another. One seller had a long table of gorgeous Provençal fabrics— tablecloths and napkins and aprons. Nell browsed but decided that wasn't what she wanted. At the far end of the market were some antiques dealers, their tables piled high with goods. She wandered among them for a while and then found what she was looking for: an antique eyelet bedspread, white with pale yellow flowers in the design, worn thin yet unmarred. She bought it.

Now, after talking to her mother in the parlor, she was hiding in the pool house, where Emily had given her scissors, a sewing kit, an iron, an ironing board, and four bamboo poles that had once been used for landscaping. She was making her mother's chuppah.

Someone knocked on the door of the pool house. She peeked outside. Fanny, who had her finger to her lips.

"I know what you're doing," she whispered. "Emily sent me to help."

Nell slid the door open and let her in, then slid it back behind her.

Fanny rubbed her wet hair wildly, a little like a dog shaking itself out. When she was done her curls fell around her ears. She's a poodle, Nell thought. An elegant poodle.

"I don't know what a chuppah is," Fanny said, "but Emily had a sneaking suspicion that you might not know how to sew."

"I have no idea how to sew," Nell said, smiling. "Thank you for saving me."

She had already cut the material but couldn't imagine how she would finish the edges. She found a chair for Fanny and put her to work.

"Where's your sister?" Fanny asked.

"I told Emily to send her out here when she woke up so my guess is that she's still sacked out."

"Brody told me that she has a very important job."

"She works too hard," Nell said. "That's for sure."

"My husband used to work too hard," Fanny said. "Sometimes I think people do that because they find it too hard to sit still."

"What do you mean?"

Nell looked at Fanny but the woman kept her eyes on the needle and thread, moving swiftly along the edge of the fabric.

"Sam wouldn't quit work. He was a doctor. Seventy-five years old and driving around the countryside, treating people who had grown up before his eyes."

"He must have loved it."

"He needed it," Fanny said. "The minute he stopped working, he lost the fire inside him."

"Why did he quit?"

"Oh, his eyesight was failing. He couldn't keep up with the technology. Even out in Wyoming, young docs were reinventing medicine and he was an old fart."

Nell laughed.

"But a person needs a life. Work shouldn't take up all the space. I tried telling him that over the years but the man is stubborn. And all he cared about was medicine."

"That doesn't seem like a bad thing," Nell said.

"Two weeks after he quit working he stopped getting out of bed. Said he was tired of life."

Nell thought of Chaney, curled in their bed, as if taking a nap. But his eyes were open.

"We think successful people are happy," Fanny said. "That's what our society fools us into believing. But my husband worked so hard as a doctor because he couldn't find comfort in a good book or a long walk. He needed work like oxygen. I don't think that's a very good way to be in the world."

Nell thought about her own life. She was very good at
being alone, reading, walking, practicing yoga. She needed to
get better at the work part of her life. She remembered Carly's
question for her yesterday: What do you do all day? She never
considered the possibility that Carly might be bad at life even
though she was so good at work.

"I heard that your husband is sick," Nell said gently.

Fanny didn't look up. "Cancer. Damn him."

"I'm sorry," Nell said.

"Well, it isn't your fault, dear. He wanted to run away and
die by himself. I took care of the man for fifty-five years and
suddenly he thinks I'm not strong enough to take care of him."

"But he wants you back," Nell said.

"He's not getting me back," Fanny said firmly.

"Because you're angry?"

Fanny straightened the fabric on her lap, then began sewing a new edge. "Women of my generation did it all wrong.
You young girls are so lucky. I was already too set in my ways
once the world began to change and women started working.
Some of my friends got jobs, got out of the house and did
something. I never wanted to. I had enough to do at the ranch
and I guess I had never given much thought to what I wanted
to do. I wanted a good husband and a child and a nice life. I got
all that. I didn't feel like I needed a career."

She stopped talking and looked at Nell, as if surprised to see
her sitting there.

"Taking care of them was your career," Nell said.

"That's right." Fanny nodded. "And then one's gone, off
to college and vet school and a whole damn life without me.

The other one wakes up one morning and says he's done with me. Gets up and walks out. After fifty-five years."

"He was too scared to tell you he was sick."

Fanny stood up. Her body swayed.

"Are you all right?" Nell asked.

"Damn him," she muttered.

"He thought he could do it without you but he can't," Nell said. "That part was your job."

Fanny sat down, smoothing her skirt over her legs. She looked around the room, her eyes finally settling on the fabric beside her.

"Hand me those scissors, dear," she said.

Nell handed them over, watching as Fanny trimmed one edge of the material and then began hemming the next side.

"I should learn to sew," Nell said.

"Why didn't your mother teach you?"

"I don't think she knows how."

"Well, grab another needle and thread," Fanny said. "I can teach you a few things."

Chapter Twenty-four

Carly stared in the mirror. She had a throbbing headache. She pulled her bottle of Advil out of her toiletry kit and took three. The glare of the bathroom light hurt her eyes.

She had dreamed of Gavin at some point during the night, a blur of a dream that had them kissing in the belly of a boat. And then the boat was sinking or she was sinking—there was water everywhere. When she opened her eyes she saw the rain on the window.

Now she brushed her teeth, remembering his tongue in her mouth, flicking in and out. She shuddered.

She found clothes to wear—jeans, a polo shirt. She had plenty of time before the wedding. For what? To make things better with Nell. To show up for her mother. To figure out her life.

What do you do when you have it all at twenty-six and suddenly you realize you have nothing at all? What do you do when you've succeeded every damn day of your life and suddenly you realize you have no skills to deal with failure?

You haven't failed, she told herself. You screwed up. Fix it.

She walked out of her room into a dark hallway. As soon as she began to walk toward the stairs, the door to another room opened. A woman appeared, a tall, voluptuous black woman, wobbling on very high heels. Her hair was piled high on her head, her makeup smeared on her face. She smiled at Carly.

"*Bonjour,*" she said.

"*Bonjour,*" Carly said.

"*Et au revoir,*" the woman said merrily and winked.

She turned and marched down the hallway, her ample butt swaying from side to side in a form-hugging miniskirt.

Carly stopped in the middle of the hallway and watched her.

"That is a lot of woman," a voice said.

Jake appeared in the doorway of his room, wearing a pair of jeans but no shirt. His chest, a young man's chest, hairless and buff, glistened with sweat. Carly looked away.

"Your date?" she asked.

"It was a very good night," he told her with a grin.

"Is she coming to the wedding?"

"God no." He laughed.

"You make it look so easy."

"Sex?" Jake asked. "Sex is easy. Relationships are fucking impossible."

"Why?"

Jake slid down the wall until he was sitting on the hallway

floor. He stretched his legs out in front of him. Carly joined him. She could smell sex on him. The whole world suddenly smelled of it.

"Sex is play," Jake said. "Love is work."

"It's that simple?"

"You in love?"

"I don't know," Carly said. "I thought I was."

"I fell in love once," Jake said, his voice a little gruff.

"What happened?"

"She married my best friend."

"Brody?"

Jake nodded. He was staring down the hallway, as if still watching the lazy swing of his date's wide hips.

"That's lousy," Carly said. "I'm sorry."

"She never knew," Jake said. "I never told her."

"Did Brody know?"

Jake shook his head. Finally he looked at Carly. "It was a lifetime ago."

"You never fell in love with another woman?"

"I never tried."

Carly stretched forward, wrapping her palms around her feet. Her body ached, her muscles strained. The body and the heart, she thought. Two separate things.

"And sex fills up all the space?"

"It does a pretty good job," Jake said, smiling. "Most days."

"You seem happy," Carly said.

"I had a nightmare last night," he said. "The woman was trying to murder me. I woke up and there she was, sacked out, a dreamy smile on her face. So why do I still feel a little haunted?"

"She gets the good time," Carly said. "I get the postcoital melancholy."

Jake laughed. "You're not a kid, are you?"

"Not really. You're not an old guy, are you?"

"Not in the least."

Jake leaned his head back against the wall and closed his eyes for a moment.

"It must be this wedding thing," Jake said, the cowboy in him turning "thing" to "thang." "My pal's getting married again. It's got me riled up somehow."

"My mom's getting married again," Carly said, her voice quiet. "It's got me riled up, too."

They heard footsteps on the stairs. Brody appeared at the end of the hallway. He stopped and stared at them. His smile disappeared in an instant and he glared at them.

"It's not what you think," Jake said, standing up.

It could have been, Carly thought. Maybe *I* spent the night in his bed. She stood up, still leaning against the wall. She could feel Jake inch away from her.

Brody walked toward them down the hall. "Carly," he said, his voice stern.

She looked up.

"Stay away from him," Brody warned.

"You're not my father," she said, suddenly sounding very young.

"I know I'm not—"

"You have no right to tell me what to do."

"We didn't do anything," Jake said. "She walked by—"

"He's old enough to be your—"

"We didn't do anything," Jake insisted.

"I care about you," Brody said, watching Carly closely.

"You don't even know me," she said, glaring back at him.

"Give me a chance to know you, then."

"Brody, you've got this all wrong," Jake said.

Brody looked at Jake and his face darkened. He put up his hands and then pushed Jake with so much force that Jake fell back onto the floor. His head slammed into the wall.

"Jesus, Brody," he moaned.

"What the hell's wrong with you?" Brody muttered.

"I didn't have sex with him!" Carly shouted. "I didn't have sex with anyone!"

Brody turned and marched down the hall. Jake stood up and stepped past her into his room, shutting the door behind him.

Carly was left in the hallway, alone.

The chef stood in the middle of the kitchen, mixing something in a bowl. He wore a white apron over his white T-shirt and jeans. His hair was pulled back into a ponytail, his face streaked with a fine dusting of flour.

"Bonjour," Carly said, entering the room and closing the door behind her.

He looked at her and a smile lit up his face. *"Buongiorno."*

"Buongiorno, Paolo," she said, remembering his name.

His brow creased with worry. "You are unhappy."

"No," she said, forcing a smile. "What are you making?"

"The cake for the marriage."

"Wedding cake!"

"My English, it is very bad."

"It's good. It's fine," Carly said. "Can I help you?"

"With wedding cake?" Paolo asked, lifting his floured hands.

"Yes," she said. "I don't know how to do a damn thing in the kitchen. I don't know how to do much of anything, it seems. I can't speak French, I can't speak Italian, I can't have a fling, I can't get along with my sister, I can't do anything except build a damn business. And you know what that business does? It's a dating service. I don't know a thing about love and somehow I'm the queen of the dating world. Does that make any sense to you?"

"Too fast," Paolo said. "I don't understand."

"Help me," Carly said so quietly that Paolo leaned toward her.

"I help you," he said, smiling.

She stepped to the sink and washed her hands, then dried them on a kitchen towel and stood at the opposite end of the center island. Paolo walked around and stood beside her. He reached for a copper bowl and placed it in front of her. It was filled with egg whites. He handed her the whisk and showed her how to move it through the liquid.

She took the whisk from him and tried to flick her wrist the way he had done. The movement was sloppy and awkward. She felt tears fill her eyes. I can't do this. I can't even beat a goddamn egg.

But then Paolo placed his hand on hers. He guided her hand gently, so that together they were whisking the eggs. She felt the heat of his palm, his breath so close to her face, his hip bone pressed against her side. She smelled vanilla. Was that him or the eggs? Her wrist found a rhythm that was fluid and easy.

He didn't step away. His hand stayed glued to hers, his body close beside her, and together they whipped until the liquid transformed into a landscape of foam, lifting into soft peaks.

Hold on, she thought. Don't let go.

Chapter Twenty-five

"I'm going to our room," Olivia said. "You have to go get dressed somewhere else."

She leaned over and kissed the top of Brody's wet head. They had finished swimming laps in the rain; Brody sat in the shallow end of the pool while Olivia gathered her already wet towel from the lounge chair.

Sébastien walked out to the meadow, hauling a big sack over his shoulder. He wore a rain poncho that made him look like a walking garbage bag.

"Why are you swimming in the storm?" he called.

"My bride had too much energy," Brody said.

"Are you complaining?" Olivia asked.

"Wouldn't think of it," Brody said. "Why do I have to get dressed somewhere else?"

"It's our wedding day. You're not supposed to see me in my dress until the wedding."

"We're not kids," Brody said. "This is an old people wedding."

"I don't know any old people getting married," Olivia said. "And my daughters want me in hiding."

"Where am I supposed to go?"

"I put your suit in Jake's room," Olivia said.

"I'm not changing in Jake's room," Brody said sharply.

"Why not? You're modest all of a sudden?"

"They were fighting," Sébastien said. He made his way around the perimeter of the pool, picking up debris from the storm and dropping it into his sack. "I heard the noise this morning."

"Fighting?" Olivia said. "You're kidding, right?"

"We weren't fighting," Brody said. "Thank you for that, Sébastien."

"*De rien,*" Sébastien said. "I had to get ice for Jake's head."

"Ice? You mean they were *physically* fighting?" Olivia asked.

"He slipped," Brody said.

"Who slipped? What are you talking about?"

"Did you see the woman he brought home last night?" Sébastien asked.

"What woman?" Olivia said.

Brody stepped out of the pool. He walked toward Sébastien.

"Some black goddess," Sébastien said. "No idea where he found her."

"What did you say?" Brody asked.

"Saw her strutting out of here this morning." Sébastien sashayed across the pool deck with an exaggerated wiggle of his hips. "*Comme ça.*"

"A black woman," Brody said.

"French," Sébastien said. "Not from around here. She needed directions to get back to town. Left her car at the port and walked to the inn with him last night."

"I'm an idiot," Brody mumbled.

Olivia glanced at him. "What did you do?"

"I've got to find Jake," Brody said, grabbing his towel and heading to the inn.

"See you at show time!" Olivia shouted.

Brody turned back and puckered his lips at her.

"No fighting!" she yelled.

She turned back to Sébastien, who wrapped up the sack and threw it over his shoulder.

"Were they really fighting?" she asked.

"I do not know a thing," Sébastien said with a smile. "I am an innocent innkeeper."

"That's about the last thing you are," Olivia muttered.

"Do not be angry with me, my friend."

"How can I not be angry?"

"I made a very bad mistake," Sébastien said. "I wish I could undo it. But I cannot."

Olivia shook her head. "Make it right, Sébastien."

"I will," he said. "I promise you."

Thunder rumbled in the distance.

"And while you're at it, can you stop this damn rain?" Olivia asked. The rain beat on her head, her shoulders, her back. She had wrapped a towel around her bathing suit but the towel, too, was damp and heavy.

"Go inside," Sébastien said. "Become a bride, *cherie*."

"Carly's better at makeup," Nell said. "We'll wait for her."

"You're sure she's up?" Olivia asked. She looked at her watch. It was already twelve-thirty.

"She's up. She was out in the hallway a while ago shouting something about sex."

"What are you talking about?" Olivia asked.

"Never mind," Nell said.

"Can you girls please try to get along today?" Olivia asked. "A little wedding gift to me?"

"We'll be fine," Nell said, though she didn't sound convinced.

Olivia stood in the doorway of her bathroom, watching Nell. She had given her the small toiletry bag in which she kept her makeup.

"This is all you have? You're worse than I am," Nell said, spreading the items on the counter.

Olivia sighed. "I'm not getting into costume to be someone else for my wedding. This is me. And I don't wear a lot of makeup."

"It's going to be you but better," Nell promised.

They heard a knock on the door.

"Carly," Olivia breathed out.

She flew to the door and opened it.

Carly stood there, wearing an apron, her arms dusted with flour.

"Who are you?" Olivia asked, laughing.

Carly smiled. "I learned how to bake a cake."

"I learned how to sew," Nell said. "It's like Home Ec 101 around here."

"I don't understand," Olivia said.

"And now we move on to the beauty portion of Emily's Finishing School for Young Women," Nell said, brandishing cosmetic brushes and pulling Olivia toward the bathroom. "Carly, you need to get your makeup kit. This is all Mom has. It's pathetic. You can do Mom's makeup, and I'll try to do something with her hair. Do something with your own hair, too. You're growing dust bunnies up there."

"It's flour," Carly said, running a hand through her hair.

"Go get your hair dryer," Nell said. "We need two in here. Suddenly I'm the only one who cares about looking good. What's wrong with you guys?"

"That's because all you have to do is mess up your hair and you look great," Olivia said, tousling Nell's hair.

"Go," Nell said to Carly, who finally turned and walked from the room.

Olivia sat in the chair in front of the small vanity in the bedroom. Nell put her hands on her shoulders. Olivia looked at her daughter in the mirror.

"It's your day, Mom," Nell said. "Let's make this a spectacular day."

Olivia felt a rush of warmth spread through her body.

Nell plugged in the hair dryer and, for a moment, Olivia closed her eyes and focused on Nell's fingers running through her hair, the heat of the dryer on her neck, the noise in her ear. Nell is taking care of me, she thought. And when she opened her eyes, she saw herself smiling in the mirror.

"How do you know how to do this?" she asked. She had to raise her voice to be heard over the roar of the dryer.

"One of my roommates is a hairstylist," Nell said. "I thought about doing that for a little while. She makes really good money. But I'd hate it. It's a very gossipy world."

"Are you thinking of giving up acting?"

Nell shook her head, then shrugged. She kept her eyes on her brush, on the lift of Olivia's hair, on the dryer expertly held in her hand. "I want to support myself," she said. "I think it's time."

"I don't mind," Olivia said. Though she did mind. It wasn't easy to send her daughter five hundred dollars a month. But she so wanted her to have a chance to make it as an actress. And she knew how hard that might be. She herself gave up too early.

"Well, I'm giving myself another month," Nell said. "Then I'm off your payroll."

Olivia reached back and patted Nell's leg. "Don't give up acting," she said. "You're too good to give it up."

"I'm not planning on giving up," Nell said. "In fact, my plan is to try harder. I've been going at it in a half-assed way. Not enough auditions. Not enough pressure on my agent. I want to change all that."

"Good for you," Olivia said. Nell looked different—she was standing taller and there was something more determined in the set of her mouth. Her Nell.

"And I think that I can still do that and get some kind of part-time job that makes enough money so I can pay my own damn rent."

Olivia watched Nell's hands in the mirror—they moved

through her hair, lifting, drying, curling. Good, she thought. I won't fight her on this one.

Olivia thought about her own decision to give up her acting career. Back in the early days she kept getting small roles in small plays—never anything that brought her real attention or satisfaction. Before her marriage to Mac she couldn't support herself as an actress so she did voice-over work for a couple of San Francisco ad companies. It all felt insignificant—she had always had such big dreams for herself. So she quit one day, early on in her marriage, and got a job as the artistic director of a regional theater company. She was probably hired because of her husband's money and connections—the nonprofit theater world wasn't immune to that—and the feminist in her always felt a little embarrassed by it. But she did the very hard work of making that theater company grow until it had real status and presence in the Bay Area arts scene. Did she miss acting? Not for a second. She had a gift for planning dynamic seasons, she had formed an accomplished resident company, and she had already created a couple of hits that went on to Broadway.

"You could come audition for a play at my theater," she suggested to Nell. She had never made the offer before. She'd always sensed that Nell needed autonomy, separation. But perhaps now she was ready. The minute the words were out of her mouth, Olivia loved the idea. "Why don't you do that?" she pressed when Nell didn't answer. "We've got a great Christopher Durang play in our next season. And there's one by a hot young female playwright that you'd love."

"I'll think about it," Nell said flatly.

"You wouldn't want to work for me?"

"I said I'll think about it," Nell repeated.

Olivia looked at herself in the mirror. Nell had transformed her hair into something new: Soft curls fell over each other, cascading down her neck.

"Wow," she said. "You're good."

"Look at you," Nell said. "You look beautiful."

"I'd really like you to think about it," Olivia said. "I know what a good actress you are."

Nell nodded, finishing Olivia's hair with a soft spray. Then she put the can on the vanity and leaned down, her face next to Olivia's. They both looked at each other in the mirror.

"San Francisco's not easy for me," Nell said. "I've got a super-lawyer father, a whiz-kid sister, and an artistic genius mom. I don't want to get lost in that. I'm just beginning to find myself apart from all of you."

Olivia nodded. "But there's something in you," she said, "that's better than all of us."

Nell kissed the top of her mother's head.

Someone knocked on the door and Nell stepped back. Olivia felt a stab of sadness that the moment ended. Already Nell was walking away and Olivia sat there, looking at her strange new self in the mirror. She had a startling thought: Somehow she always felt that supporting Nell financially kept her wayward daughter tied to her. Nell always felt so easy to lose, as if Olivia might turn her back and her daughter would slip away. But it occurred to her now that the opposite might be true. By letting her go, her daughter might come back to her.

"Man, you've got a lot of makeup," she heard Nell say to Carly in the other room.

"I'm useless with makeup," Olivia called out to them. "You'll have to do it for me."

"That's the plan," Nell said. She bustled into the room, setting up the bathroom stool next to the desk chair. "You sit here," she ordered Carly, pointing at the stool. "Now transform this woman into a bride."

Carly sat. For a moment she stared at Olivia as if looking at a blank canvas. Where are you? Olivia wanted to say.

"Color," Carly said. "You need color."

"What's wrong?" Olivia said quietly.

"I need to concentrate," Carly told her. "You need to hold your face still."

"Grrr," Olivia said, scrunching her face.

"And no faces," Carly said.

She set to work, smoothing a foundation on Olivia's face, adding bronzer and blush, working all kinds of products on her eyes. Olivia loved the feeling of Carly's hands on her face, smudging, rubbing, tapping. But she watched her daughter's own face and saw a dark sadness there. She wanted to push the brushes and pots and creams away and take Carly in her arms. But she kept quiet, kept still and let herself be pampered.

"*Et voilà,*" Carly said, leaning back.

"Can I look?" Olivia asked.

Carly nodded.

Olivia turned toward the mirror. The woman looking back at her surprised her; she smiled at her reflection. "Why have I spent my life looking drab when I could have wowed the world with this face?" she asked.

"Drab," Nell moaned. "No one would ever describe my mother as drab."

"But this is magic," Olivia whispered, peering at her smoky eyes, her long lashes, her contoured cheekbones.

"Wowza," Nell said, appearing at her side. "It's a bride!"

"Thank you," Olivia said to both girls.

"Into your dress now!" Nell commanded.

"My god, you two are taskmasters," Olivia said, smiling.

"We learned from a pro," Nell said. "Look over here, *madame*." She gestured into the bedroom.

Olivia saw that her wedding dress—a silk dress with a vivid print of melting roses—was spread across the bed. But Nell was pointing in the other direction. Olivia noticed her smile and followed her arm. Was she pointing at something on the wall? Near the wall? And then she saw the window that was filled with brilliant sunshine.

"You've got yourself a wedding day," Nell said.

Olivia stepped toward her and took her hand. "You even managed this," she said breathlessly.

"Let's get you dressed," Nell said. "Your groom is waiting."

Chapter Twenty-six

The grass was soaking wet. Nell stepped outside and immediately her high heels sunk into the soft turf.

Emily joined her and moaned. "This isn't going to work."

"We'll go barefoot," Nell suggested.

"You're nuts," Emily told her.

They both faced the garden. Sébastien had cleaned the area of debris from the storm and now the lavender, hyacinth, and poppies glistened in the sunshine. The sky, a vivid blue, was washed clean of clouds. Drops of rainwater on the leaves of the olive trees caught the sun and sent out sparkles.

"It's perfect," Nell said.

"Except that we can't walk across the grass. What the hell do we do?"

"I'm serious," Nell said. "No one will wear shoes. My mother was a hippie once. It's a barefoot wedding."

Nell tossed off her shoes and started walking up the path to the garden.

"It feels great!" she called back. The wet grass tickled her feet.

She was carrying the chuppah tucked under one arm, the eyelet material now sewn with clean edges and tied to the bamboo poles. She wore a pale yellow sundress, with spaghetti straps and a fitted bodice. Who cared about shoes?

In the center of the garden she found the spot where she wanted to set up the chuppah. She laid it down on a table and turned around, imagining the guests gathered beneath it. She felt nervous and excited—she couldn't tell which emotion churned in her stomach. She looked back at Emily, who was still standing in place, her heels mired in the wet earth.

"Oh, come on," Nell called. "Take the damn things off and get over here!"

Emily shrugged, pulled off her shoes and tentatively took a few steps. Then she giggled. "Feels so funny," she said. She walked hesitantly toward Nell in the garden.

"Well, I guess your mother will have a hippie wedding," she said.

"Do you have any idea if Jake will take the ceremony seriously?" Nell asked. She knew that her mother wasn't crazy about the idea of Brody's party-boy pal performing their ceremony. Jake had gotten his license online and Brody had promised that he'd do a good job. But as far as Nell could tell, the guy didn't take much seriously.

"He doesn't exactly seem like the minister type," Emily said, "unless ministers are really into six-pack abs these days."

"He is pretty hot for an old guy," Nell said.

"Stay away from him," Emily warned.

"Oh, I have no plans to fool around with anyone anytime soon."

"You doing all right?"

"Yeah," Nell said. "Gavin was a mistake I won't repeat."

"Let's go tell everyone we're having a barefoot wedding," Emily said.

Nell rapped on Carly's door. When the door finally swung open, Carly stood there, wearing a green dress, her hair hanging limply to her shoulders.

"Damn," Nell said. "Into the bathroom. I'll put your hair up. But we're late. We've got like two minutes before we're all supposed to meet in the garden."

"I'm fine," Carly said. "You don't have to do this for me."

"You look like hell." Nell marched her into the bathroom and sat her down at the vanity. She pulled Carly's hair up and twisted it into a knot at the back of her head, pinning it in place. She freed some strands from the bun and let them fall along the side of her face. "Better," she said. "Let's go."

Carly sat there.

"It's mom's wedding day. Let's do this for her."

Carly nodded, and Nell let out a long sigh.

"I don't know what you did with him and I don't care."

"I shouldn't have gotten into the car with him. I had some idea that—"

"Why'd you call me, Carly? Why couldn't you have taken a cab back from Marseille? I never would have suspected that you did whatever the hell you did. But you wanted me to know. Why?"

Carly hung her head. "I'm falling apart."

"You don't fall apart. The rest of the world falls apart and you just keep on working."

"Maybe I can't do it anymore."

"Take a fucking time-out, then. You've been on your game every day of your life. Hit the sidelines. Be a slacker."

"A slacker," Carly said dreamily.

"I spent my childhood listening to Mom and Dad talk about the brilliant and astonishing Carly Levin. You have a lot to live up to, sister. I've got the easy job. No one expects much of me except a few more fuck-ups along the way." She looked at her watch. "And if we're late for this wedding it will be my fault. Not yours. So let's move it."

Nell turned and walked out of the bathroom. She could hear Carly blow her nose. And then the sound of her footsteps followed Nell down the hall and out of the house.

When they got to the garden, Fanny, Jake, Sébastien, and Emily were gathered there, all shoeless. The men had their pants rolled up to their ankles. Ulysse stood at Emily's side, his tail wagging.

"I love it," Nell said. "Hillbilly wedding."

"You girls look beautiful," Fanny said.

"Thanks," they both said at once.

"I needed Nell's help," Carly said, smiling.

"Listen, here's the plan," Nell said. "This is a chuppah." She lifted the material and bamboo rods from the table. "It's a

Jewish tradition. I even found out what it means. It represents the home that the couple will create together. We hold it above them, like a canopy. Fanny, you'll hold one pole, Emily will hold another, Carly and I will hold the other ones. Mom and Brody will stand underneath it during the ceremony."

"Where do I stand?" Jake asked.

Nell thought of saying, "In the swimming pool." But she shrugged and said, "In front of them. I don't know if there's room under the chuppah or if you're supposed to be in there. So we'll wing it on that one."

"You made this?" Carly asked. She reached up and touched the antique fabric with her fingertips.

"I had a little help from Fanny," Nell said.

"She found the material at the farmers' market this morning," Emily told them.

"It's amazing," Carly said, looking up as they all took the poles and spread the material above their heads.

"I'll go get the groom," Sébastien said.

"Turn on the music!" Emily called after him.

Nell could feel her heart racing.

"You did a wonderful thing," Fanny said. "I love this hookah."

Nell and Carly burst out laughing. Nell reached over and touched Fanny's arm. "It's a chuppah, Fanny. A hookah gets you stoned. A chuppah gets you married."

"I'm very confused," Fanny said, but she, too, grinned widely.

"My best friend's getting married," Emily said. They all looked at her. "In my garden. Look at this. Look at us."

Jazz music filled the garden from speakers hidden in the

nooks of the trees. Nell couldn't identify the song but she loved the sound of the flute, as clear and lilting as a bird's call.

"Look at that happy guy," Jake said.

They all turned toward the house. Brody had kicked off his shoes and rolled up the pant legs of his suit. He was marching down the path toward them, beaming.

"You stand right under the canopy," Nell told him.

"It's a chuppah," Fanny said.

Brody leaned over to kiss Nell, then Carly, then Fanny and Emily. He stepped under the chuppah.

Sébastien joined them, standing behind Emily and Ulysse. Nell saw him touch Emily's lower back, but she inched away. Sébastien's hand drifted back to his side.

The music changed to something lovely and slow—a woman singing words in a language that Nell couldn't identify—and they all turned toward the house again to see Olivia appear at the door.

She looked beautiful in her dress of roses, her hair falling in waves onto her neck. She lifted one bare foot and placed it carefully in the grass. Then she stepped forward with the other. She looked toward them in the garden, taking in the chuppah, the group of them watching her, the music and sunshine and the field of wildflowers, and she paused for a second to wipe at the corner of her eye. Standing there watching her, Nell noticed that her own rapidly beating heart had found an easier rhythm. Her mother was getting married.

Olivia walked toward them along the path, her smile spread from ear to ear. The late-afternoon light was silver and bright, casting long shadows.

When she reached the girls, Olivia leaned forward and kissed them each in turn.

"Stand under the chuppah," Nell whispered. "Right next to your guy."

"The chuppah," Olivia said, her voice quiet. She looked up. Nell followed her gaze. The eyelet material let the sun shine through, sending down pinpoints of light. "Thank you," her mother whispered.

She stepped to Brody's side and he took her hand.

"You're the most beautiful woman I've ever seen," he whispered, and Nell felt her own heart fill.

Jake cleared his throat. He stood in front of the couple, just outside the chuppah. Should he be inside? Nell wished she had done a little more research. It doesn't matter—does it? Suddenly she was nervous again. Why would Brody have chosen this guy to perform the wedding ceremony?

"I'm honored that my best friend asked me to officiate," Jake said. "I'm not the obvious choice—I've avoided commitment all my life. Brody knows that. He also knows that I know him like a brother. And that as much as I need to run free this guy needs to share his life with someone he loves. Luckily, he's found that someone, and I've never seen him happier. I've never seen him choose love over work and Wyoming and his horses. And now that I've gotten to know Olivia I understand how this happened. This tiny person in front of me is so much bigger than work and Wyoming and horses. She offers him love and two daughters. She opens her heart and says come on in. That's big love.

"And I'm envious for the first time. I want some of that. I

can imagine what it might be like to share your life with someone when that person makes you so damn happy. Look at us here. We're all just about bursting at the seams because your love spills over the top and finds its way into our own hearts.

"So this thing you're standing under is a chuppah, I'm told. It represents the home that you'll build together. But take a look at one thing. It's held up by Brody's mother, by Olivia's best friend, and by your two new daughters. That's what holds your home. You've got your family and closest friends holding you close and building a foundation for that new marriage."

He paused and cleared his throat. "Ladies and gentlemen. We are gathered here today to witness . . . my debut as a wedding officiant."

Everyone laughed. Jake smiled and took a deep breath.

"I'm going to read this next part so I don't mess up. It wasn't easy getting my online certificate of ministry from the Universal Life Church."

Jake read from a paper in his hand. "By the power invested in me by the State of Wyoming," he said, and he raced through the rest of the official declaration.

He stopped reading and looked at Brody and Olivia. Nell looked, too. The couple stared into each other's eyes, their faces lit by the sun piercing the canopy above them. They held each other's hands, Brody's long fingers wrapped around Olivia's. Nell could smell jasmine and something else—dog breath. Ulysse pushed up against her leg, trying to find a spot for himself under the chuppah.

Jake started to say something and his voice broke. He wiped his eyes with the back of his hand. "I better wrap this up before I make a fool of myself."

Nell saw that everyone had tears in their eyes.

"Would you kiss your bride already and get us some champagne?" he said, and everyone laughed as Brody took Olivia's face in his hands. They looked at each other for a moment and then they kissed, long and hard.

Chapter Twenty-seven

"Can I borrow your phone?" Carly asked Nell.

They were still gathered in the garden, champagne glasses in hand. Carly felt unmoored. She had found herself moved by her mother's wedding ceremony despite herself. She still didn't particularly want Brody in her life. Like a child, she wanted her father at her mother's side. But Carly had never seen her parents gaze into each other's eyes the way Olivia and Brody did.

"Where's yours?" Nell asked with a frown.

"I left it in my room," Carly said, surprised. She hadn't even thought about bringing it down with her.

"You calling Gavin?" Nell asked, a bitter note in her voice.

"No!" Carly said, too loud. Emily and Jake, who were

standing nearby, turned to look at her. She stepped away from them.

"I have to call Wes," she told Nell more softly.

"You going to tell him what happened?"

"Leave me alone, Nell," Carly said. "You said we could drop this for a few hours. So drop it."

Nell pulled her phone out of her clutch and passed it over. "Everyone's going to make their toasts in a few minutes," she said. "Don't disappear."

"I won't," Carly promised.

She took the phone and walked away from the gathering, tapping in Wes's cell number.

"Nell?" Wes answered, his voice thick with sleep.

"I need to talk to you," Carly said.

She wandered around the house and toward the pool. Her bare feet were soaked from the wet grass. She stepped over a fallen branch; something sharp pricked her heel. She couldn't feel the pain of it, but when she lifted her foot, she saw blood dripping from a cut. She lowered her foot and kept walking.

"I'm trying to sleep," Wes said. "Can this wait?"

"No," Carly said. She looked at the lounge chairs—they were all drenched with rainwater. So she paced the perimeter of the pool.

"Where were you yesterday?" Wes asked.

"Nowhere," she said.

"You're always somewhere," Wes said. "I bet you've never played hooky one day in your life."

"That's what I did yesterday, Wes," she said. "I played hooky."

"What's going on, Carly?"

"I'm quitting."

"Quitting what?"

Carly turned around. She saw a trail of bloodstained foot-prints on the tile around the pool. She followed her own foot-prints in reverse.

"Work. You. I'm done."

"You want to call me later?" Wes asked. "I must be having a bad dream. Let's talk when I've had some coffee."

"No," Carly said. "I want to do it now."

"Do what now?"

"Doug Barnes can replace me temporarily. He's good enough. Until you hire someone else."

"You have a replacement set up for my girlfriend, too?"

"You're on your own for that one," Carly said.

"Someone hired you. Unique made you an offer. Castaway. Who's hiring you?"

"No one's hiring me."

"You're starting your own company. Why am I not sur-prised?" Wes sounded disgusted.

"You're wrong," Carly said. "I'm just getting out. I need a break."

"So take a break. It's called a sabbatical. We can take a rela-tionship sabbatical, too, if you want one. What the hell hap-pened over there?"

"I gotta go, Wes. Sorry to dump this all on you. But I had to. I'll talk to you when I'm back in town. I've got to go. My mother's wedding and all."

"Fuck you, Carly."

She hung up the phone, then stopped pacing and looked

around. The sunlight glimmered on the pool, on the wet tiles, on the rain-soaked umbrellas. Carly lifted her sunglasses and watched the world brighten.

"I'd like to make a toast!" Emily called, clinking a fork against her champagne glass.

Carly walked quickly to the center of the garden to join the group. Her heel had stopped bleeding but now her feet were covered with mud, and when she looked at her legs, she also saw scratches across her shins.

She grabbed a glass of champagne from the table and passed the phone back to her sister, then stood at her side.

"What the hell?" Nell said, looking at Carly's legs.

"Shhh," everyone said at once.

"My best friend just got hitched," Emily said. She walked to Olivia's side and threw one arm around her. "And I couldn't be happier."

Olivia leaned over and kissed Emily's cheek.

"But listen up," Emily began. "Right now you're in heaven. Right now you guys are thinking this marriage thing is as easy as breathing."

"Don't," Olivia said, stepping away from Emily.

"Trust me on this one," Emily whispered.

Olivia looked at her doubtfully. Sébastien took a step closer to his wife but he, too, looked wary. Why? Carly wondered.

"Marriage is complicated," Emily said. "Marriage is messy." She glanced at Sébastien. "Sometimes very messy." She turned back to Olivia and Brody. "But love—love gets you through the tough parts. It makes you a better human being. Love helps lift us above our own frailties and enables us to soar." She lifted her glass to the bride and groom. "Here's to the remarkable gift of love. And now let's feast."

The three of them shared clinks and kisses but Sébastien held back.

While everyone else made their way around the house toward the arbor, Carly watched Sébastien approach Emily.

"Je t'aime," he said, taking her hands in his. "I love our marriage. I will do everything I can so that you can trust me again."

Emily glanced at Carly. "You didn't hear that."

"I didn't hear a thing," Carly said.

"Go eat," Emily said. "That's an order."

"Oui, madame."

As Carly walked around the house toward the noise of all the other guests, she glanced behind her. Emily and Sébastien were kissing.

He cheated on her? Carly thought. Impossible. Was the myth of Emily really a myth? During all the years of Carly's parents' bad marriage, Carly had counted on Emily and Sébastien as the ones who did it right. Maybe no one did it right. Or maybe even a perfect life has broken moments.

The arbor was draped with white lights, woven through the wisteria. Emily had set a beautiful table, with flowers floating in glass bowls, a panel of antique lace running down the center. How had Carly paced the perimeter of the pool so many times while talking to Wes and failed to notice the table? I'm sleepwalking, Carly thought. I used to be the one who took it all in at a glance. Now I can't see a step in front of me.

Everyone gathered around, murmuring compliments about

the lovely table. Carly watched Nell straighten Brody's tie. She's the good sister, Carly thought. She loved the guy the minute Olivia introduced him to them. I've been bitching about the cowboy without ever talking to him. It turns out I'm the fuck-up, the loser.

Paolo walked out of the back door of the inn and called to all of them. "It is dinner now!"

He wore a white chef's jacket over his jeans. Without his ponytail, his hair fell in waves onto his shoulders. His piercing blue eyes sought her out, and he smiled. She thought of his hand on hers, moving the whisk through the egg whites.

"Dinner!" Olivia called.

"Bring on the wedding feast!" Brody proclaimed.

Carly considered following Paolo into the kitchen. But everyone moved toward the table, so she took a seat next to Nell. Fanny sat on her other side.

"I'd like to say something, too," Brody said. He walked up to Olivia and slipped an arm around her waist.

He raised his glass. "I'm not a guy who likes to give a speech," he said, clearing his throat. "In Wyoming I had my big country and my simple life. My first wife, Grace, and I didn't have kids. So we had horses and dogs. Not a bad thing. But I went to work and when I came home I worked the ranch, keeping myself busy. I thought I was happy—I suppose I was happy. But I've come to learn a different kind of happiness. When I met Olivia my life went from black and white to Technicolor. I now have two daughters whom I already love. And I have a wife who lives life on a grand stage."

Everyone laughed; Olivia elbowed Brody.

"My heart had to grow to make room for this very big life.

I never knew love could take up so much space. And this is exactly the way I want it to be. Olivia, my bride. Thank you for marrying me."

When they kissed, Carly could feel her eyes fill with tears.

Sometime in the middle of dinner, Carly sneaked away from the table. She walked into the kitchen and found Paolo at the sink, washing dishes. He didn't see her standing there. She watched him for a moment. His face was serious, his brow creased with concentration. I don't know what he's thinking, she thought. I don't even know if he's smart. I don't know a thing about him.

"I can help," she said.

He turned around.

"You are here," he said, his eyes widening. "I think about you, and then you are here."

"Magic," she said.

"You are hurt," he said, looking at her feet.

She shook her head. One foot was still smeared with blood. "It's a mess," she told him, "but I'll survive. I stepped on something."

He walked up to her, drying his hands on the towel tucked into the waist of his apron.

"Here," he said, pointing to a stool.

She sat at the center island.

He kneeled down and lifted her foot. His hand was warm on her skin and yet she felt a shiver run through her body. He examined her foot, pressing softly on her skin. She closed her eyes, letting his touch quiet the thoughts in her mind. And then he let her go. She opened her eyes.

He returned to the sink and ran water over a fresh hand towel. Then he sat on the floor with her foot in his lap. His touch was gentle, soothing. He washed the top of her foot and then carefully moved the towel over her sole. At one point she flinched with pain.

"*Scusi,*" he said. "I clean it."

She nodded, watching him.

He cleaned the cut and then dried it with a fresh towel. He found ointment to put on it and then taped a bandage over it. When he was done, he brought her foot to his mouth and kissed her instep.

She reached out and touched his head.

He sat back and looked at her, and she smiled.

"*Sì,*" she whispered, and he leaned forward, pressing his lips against hers. As they kissed, she heard a humming sound inside her head, a sound that she had never heard before. It poured through her as if it were liquid and soon she felt as if she were floating in it.

Together, they stood up, and she leaned into him and they kept kissing, and all the words in her brain disappeared.

"Excuse me," Carly heard and she stepped back, surprised.

She looked toward the door where Brody stood, smiling.

"I'm sorry," he said. "I didn't mean—"

"We just—" Carly said. "I don't know how I got this cut." She lifted her foot and held it in the air. Ridiculous, she thought. She put it down and stood there. She could still hear the soft humming sound inside her.

"I cook," Paolo said, moving toward the back of the kitchen.

"I was coming to get more wine."

"My foot—I stepped on something—"

"Please, Carly," Brody said. "I don't care. I'm not going to deck anyone. I thought that Jake had—I don't know—you're a beautiful young woman and I thought he was taking advantage—"

"I can take care of myself," she said.

"I was mad at Jake," Brody said. "He's an old guy who shouldn't be—"

"He didn't do anything."

"I know that now. I'm sorry."

They stood there, looking at each other. Somewhere behind them Paolo was chopping something, the sound of the knife clicking rapidly.

"I don't need a new father," Carly said, lifting her chin.

"So I'm just your mom's husband," Brody said, an easy smile on his face. "We start there."

"I don't even know you."

"We've got plenty of time for that," Brody said. "The rest of our lives."

Carly nodded. "You guys look really happy. My dad wasn't very good at making Mom happy."

Brody didn't say anything for a moment. "She makes me very happy, too," he finally said.

"Did you hurt Jake?"

Brody shook his head. "The guy has a pretty thick skull."

"He was in love with . . ." Carly said, trailing off.

Brody nodded. "With Grace. I knew that. He was kind of a puppy dog around her."

Carly smiled. "Somehow I can't imagine Jake as a puppy dog."

"He puts on a good act."

"And he's never fallen in love with anyone else."

"He's scared, I think," Brody said.

"Of what?"

"Of what happens when you open your heart."

"Me, too," Carly said.

Brody walked toward her. She watched him, wondering what he would say. Tell me, she thought. Tell me what to do.

But he just opened his arms and she stepped in.

Chapter Twenty-eight

Olivia stood at the edge of the patio and watched the guests dancing under the white lights that were strung from tree to tree. Carly and Nell danced together, both of them distracted, looking everywhere except at each other. Nell was the good dancer, graceful and fluid in her movements. Carly's arms jerked awkwardly; her feet shuffled without rhythm. Lucky thing she's so smart, Olivia thought. Then Nell pulled Carly close and whispered in her ear.

Carly nodded, then closed her eyes. She stood, her body swaying to the music. Slowly she began to dance with her eyes closed. And sure enough, she found a rhythm and began to move in time to the music. She opened her eyes and laughed out loud. Nell high-fived her. Look at that, Olivia thought, smiling.

Nearby, Brody was dancing with Fanny. He twirled his mother under his arm. They looked elegant and happy, two tall herons on the dance floor. When the dance ended, Fanny curtsied, and Brody kissed her hand.

A new song began; Sébastien and Emily stepped onto the patio. It was a slow dance, and Sébastien put his arms around his wife. She rested her cheek in the crook of his neck and they swayed together, their bodies close.

Please get through this, Olivia thought.

Suddenly Fanny was at her side, laughing. "What a wonderful party," she said. They watched Brody ask Carly to dance. She hesitated—Olivia knew that her daughters weren't very good at ballroom dancing. Even *she* was lousy at following a man's lead—maybe it was a genetic trait.

But Carly apparently agreed because Brody took one of her hands in his and placed the other on the small of her back. He whispered in her ear.

"I think he's teaching her how to dance," Olivia said.

"She doesn't know how?" Fanny asked.

"Their generation doesn't slow dance, I think. In fact, all I ever learned was the bear hug."

"Well, you'll learn now," Fanny said.

They watched as Brody and Carly moved tentatively across the dance floor.

"Apparently he's a good teacher," Olivia said.

"I changed my flight," Fanny said, turning to face her. "I already told Brody. I've got a taxi picking me up in a half hour."

"Why?"

"I want to get back to my husband," Fanny said. "I think it's time."

"Oh, I'm so glad to hear that."

Fanny sighed deeply. "I know my Sam. He spent his whole life taking care of the rest of the world. He was a wonderful doctor."

"I'm sure he was."

"And he can't imagine that someone might take care of him."

Olivia nodded. "I've heard that doctors make the worst patients."

"This is what it means to love someone," Fanny said. "After so many years. It's what you do in the end."

"I wish he could have been here."

"At least I'll be going home to him."

Olivia smiled. "The thought of that makes me very happy."

"First, though, I'm going to give him hell," Fanny said, a corner of her mouth lifting in a grin. "And then I'll put on my Florence Nightingale cap and do what I have to do."

"It will be hard," Olivia said.

"But we'll be together," Fanny told her.

Olivia leaned over and gave her a kiss. "I'm so glad you were here, Fanny."

"Me, too."

"Don't be mad at me for taking Brody away from you and Wyoming."

"You are the best thing that ever happened to that boy," Fanny said, and then she squeezed Olivia's shoulder before starting to walk back to the inn.

Olivia watched her go, thinking about Grace, long gone. I have no reason to be jealous of you, she thought. You kept him happy for a long time. Now it's my turn.

She turned back to the dance floor to see Brody swing Carly under his arm. Carly was so surprised that she let out a quick laugh.

Olivia laughed, too, standing alone, watching her family.

"Let them eat cake!" Emily shouted from the kitchen door.

Everyone turned around and watched Paolo emerge, carrying a large cake on a white platter.

Olivia grabbed Brody's hand and walked toward the arbor. The dinner table had been cleared and Paolo set the cake in the center. White and red buttercream roses, the same shade as Olivia's dress, covered the top of the cake.

"It's gorgeous!" Olivia said.

Paolo beamed. *"Grazie,"* he said, glancing shyly in Carly's direction.

The guests gathered around while Olivia and Brody cut the first slice of cake. Then Paolo took over, cutting and offering slices to everyone.

"More champagne!" Sébastien shouted, popping the cork from another bottle. He refilled everyone's glasses.

Nell walked over to Olivia, plate in one hand, champagne glass in the other.

"It's my turn for a toast!" she called out to the guests.

Olivia felt a burst of pleasure—she hadn't thought that Nell would make a toast. Normally, it would have been Carly who would step up and speak. Good for Nell, Olivia thought. It's her turn.

"I'm amazed," Nell said, her voice loud and strong. "It's no surprise that my mother would wrangle the cutest damn cowboy in America and make him her own. It's no surprise that Emily and Sébastien would throw open their doors and let us celebrate in this lovely spot. No—I'm amazed by love. I'm amazed by the force of it, the enormous power of it. Can't you feel it? It's as if Olivia and Brody's love wraps around all of us. We're bathing in it. It's the light of the moon. I feel stronger and happier because of their love. And it makes me yearn for some of that magic myself."

Nell turned to Olivia.

"Thanks for teaching me so much throughout the years. And this lesson, the way it feels to love someone, might be the most important of all."

Olivia felt tears running down her cheeks. She stepped forward and hugged Nell.

"To love!" Nell shouted when Olivia released her. She lifted her champagne glass in the air.

"To love!" all the guests shouted in return.

Carly, her eyes wet, looked at her mother and mouthed the words. "To love."

Later, Olivia sat at the edge of the pool, her feet dangling in the water. Her daughters were dancing again, and this time Paolo joined them. Brody and Jake sat across from each other at the dining-room table, drinking beer. Sébastien and Emily had disappeared into their room, hand in hand. Olivia was thinking about dragging Brody away. She wanted to take him to bed. Soon.

She watched as Nell walked away from the patio, leaving Carly and Paolo dancing together. Nell headed toward the pool, a broad smile on her face.

"Can I sit with you?"

"I'd love that," Olivia said.

Nell took a seat next to her and dipped her feet in the water. "Oh, that feels so good on my poor dancing feet," she said with a sigh.

"Look at them," Olivia said, gesturing to Carly and Paolo.

"Sweet, huh," Nell said.

"That's the kind of guy Carly needs. Not a brainiac. A man with a heart."

"I was thinking the same thing," Nell said. "That's why I sneaked away."

Carly and Paolo danced around each other. Paolo was beaming, so clearly smitten by his partner. Carly kept her eyes on him and moved with a new grace. She seemed to be following his rhythm, their bodies so in sync that it looked as if they were connected by invisible threads.

When the song ended, Carly glanced at Olivia and Nell, then said something to Paolo. He stepped close to her and kissed her cheek. She lowered her head, the first sign of shyness that Olivia had ever seen in her daughter. And then Carly walked over to where they were sitting at the far end of the pool.

"Can I join you guys?" she asked, and they both nodded.

She sat on the other side of Olivia and dropped her legs into the pool.

"Cute guy," Nell said.

"Cute guy," Carly murmured.

The three of them sat there quietly for a while, their feet dangling in the cool water. Paolo cleared the dessert dishes.

Jake and Brody clinked beer bottles and roared with laughter. The lights swung in the breeze, their reflection glittering in the swimming pool.

"There's a story I want to tell you," Carly said quietly.

Both Olivia and Nell turned toward her. They waited. Carly watched her own feet drifting slowly back and forth in the water.

"When we were in high school," Carly said, glancing at Olivia, then looking away just as quickly. "Remember the time that Nell got arrested?"

"Of course," Olivia said. She wanted to stop her daughter: Why bring that up now? Why ruin a good moment? We're here, aren't we? We made it through that disaster a long time ago.

But Carly went on. "Something else happened that night. Something different from the story you know."

"Carly," Nell said. "Don't."

"Don't what?" Olivia asked.

"Let me talk," Carly insisted.

Both Olivia and Nell fell silent. They angled their bodies so they could watch Carly, but she kept her eyes on her feet, as if she were telling her story from somewhere far away.

"There was a party at Christine's before the dance. Someone gave me a bottle of pills and I took one of them—I don't know why I did it. I was tired of being the good girl all the time. I didn't even know what kind of pill it was. Everyone else was taking it. Now I'm guessing it was Ecstasy but who knows—could have been anything."

She stopped talking for a moment and Olivia thought about

that night. She remembered Carly going right to her room after she picked her up. She was sick, Olivia had thought. But high? Olivia had never even considered the possibility. If it had been Nell she would have suspected as much right away. But not Carly.

"When I got to the dance the drug must have kicked in because suddenly I was very high. Someone gave me a flask and I drank whatever was in there. I thought it would bring me down a little—I didn't know anything about how drugs and alcohol worked."

"You still don't know anything," Nell said.

Carly nodded. "Pretty soon I was wasted. I don't remember much except for dancing with some guys I didn't even know. And then my superhero sister showed up."

"And I took you home and put you to bed," Nell said. "End of story."

"Not the end of the story," Carly said. She glanced at her mother. "I want you to hear the end of the story."

"I'm listening," Olivia said. She was beginning to feel the truth sneak up on her. Her memories of that night were unlocking, new images tumbling into place.

"Nell dragged me out of there and drove me home," Carly said. "The cops pulled us over. I don't even know why."

"They said I rolled a stop sign," Nell said. "They were just looking for high school kids to hassle."

"Nell was wearing my jean jacket. The cops found the pills," Carly said. She splashed the water with her feet and then held them still. "Nell said they were hers."

Olivia let silence fall between them for a moment. She

imagined the night, remembered the phone call and conjured up the anger that she so often felt toward Nell. She could almost taste something bitter in her mouth.

"Why, Nell?" she asked.

Nell shrugged. "Carly had too much to lose. It was right before she started the Google internship. She was up for that debate scholarship. I wasn't going to let her miss out on all that."

"My God," Olivia said. "You took the fall for her."

"It wasn't such a big deal," Nell said. Now she, too, was looking at her feet, flexing and pointing them on the surface of the water.

"It was a big deal," Olivia said. "You got kicked out of school. UC Santa Cruz rescinded their acceptance at first."

"Yeah. Whatever."

"Nell," Olivia said. "Look at me."

"Why do I feel like I'm in trouble again?" Nell said. She turned up one side of her mouth as if she were making a joke.

"You're most definitely not in trouble," Olivia said. "I can't believe you did that."

Again, Nell shrugged.

"And I always pretended I couldn't remember what happened," Carly said. "We never talked about it."

"Why?" Olivia asked.

"Because I didn't know what to do with it. I owed her too much. I felt like a lousy sister. I felt like a fraud."

"You did what you had to do," Nell said. "You succeeded. You thrived. You got to have your brilliant career that you were meant to have."

"And you?" Olivia asked.

"I'll get there," Nell said. "I'm just on a slower track. It didn't change my life irrevocably."

"You didn't go to college," Olivia said. "You were all set to go."

"Maybe I wasn't ready," Nell said.

"Attention all women!" Jake called from the table under the arbor.

The three of them lifted their heads at once and looked at Jake and Brody across the lawn.

"Charge!" Jake shouted. The two men stood up and raced each other, drunkenly, to the pool. They both cannonballed in, hitting the water at the same time.

The water splashed Olivia and her daughters, who leaned back, laughing. The guys whooped and whistled.

"Boys," Olivia muttered.

"Come on in!" Jake shouted.

"I'm so glad I had girls," Olivia said, putting her arms around her daughters.

"I'm not done," Carly said quietly.

Olivia dropped her arms. She looked at Brody and Jake, bobbing in the center of the pool.

"Let us finish this conversation," she told them.

Both men peeled off their wet shirts and threw them to the side of the pool.

"Go ahead," Olivia said. "I'm listening."

"Thank you, Nell," Carly said. "I should have done this a very long time ago."

"You don't need to—" Nell started.

"I do. Listen. Thank you for saving my ass back when I was sixteen. I owe you—"

"You don't owe me anything."

"She can't listen," Carly complained to Olivia.

"Shut up and listen to your sister," Olivia said, smiling.

"I owe you so much," Carly said. Her voice broke. "I wasn't big enough to tell you what it meant to me."

She stopped, and they were all quiet for a moment.

"I hear you," Nell said, nodding.

Olivia caught a glimpse of the moon, a shining crescent in the night sky. It looked like a lopsided smile, grinning at her. Lucky me, she thought, smiling right back.

Ulysse barked from across the pool and Brody tossed him a soggy tennis ball, far across the meadow. The dog happily bounded after it.

Nell dropped into the pool. Her dress floated up around her. She walked past Olivia and stopped in front of Carly. Then she reached out her hand and Carly, too, slipped into the pool and into her sister's arms.

Olivia opened her eyes and saw the first sign of dawn. Rose-colored light filled the room. They hadn't gone to bed until after two—she needed more sleep. But she needed Brody first.

She ran her hand along the length of his side, his hip, his thigh.

He murmured and turned toward her. "Is it morning?"

"Not yet," she said.

He put his arm on her back and moved his fingers in slow, lazy circles on her skin.

"We're married," he said.

"We're married," she agreed, smiling. She reached out and ran her hand along the side of his face.

"It was wonderful," he said. Their faces were close to each other on the pillow; their voices were whispers.

"It was wonderful," she told him.

"We didn't consummate our marriage last night," he murmured.

"Then we better get on it."

"Promise me that we have nothing else to do today," he said, his mouth close to hers.

"Everyone's leaving today," Olivia told him. "We have the whole day to ourselves."

"I like that," Brody said. "Come closer."

"I can't get any closer," she said.

"I don't believe that," he said, rolling his body on top of hers.

She loved the weight of him, the smell of him. "Is this what marriage is?" she asked. "This? The two of us right now?"

"Yes," he said. "And it's every moment after this."

"Well then," she said, wrapping her legs around him. "Good morning, my husband," she whispered, burying her face in his neck.

"Good morning, my wife," he said.

Acknowledgments

First I'd like to thank my daughters, Gillian and Sophie. They know they are not Nell and Carly, but they're going to get asked a lot of questions about my characters and any possible resemblance to them. Thanks for understanding that writers make stuff up, including twentysomething daughters. Thanks for putting up with the questions. Here's the one part of the fictional mother-daughter relationship that's absolutely true: Love. Big love.

Maison 9, a small inn in Cassis, France, is not La Maison Verte. But I stayed there twice, and my imaginary inn grew from the beauty and charm of that wonderful place. Many thanks to Christel Soria-Goossens, inn manager, for all that you do to create the magic at Maison 9. And thanks to Yann

Chauveau, owner of the very real restaurant on the beach, Le Bada, for treating us so well while we were there.

Many thanks to Tom Brown, Jr., of Grouper, for answering my questions about dating websites and start-ups. Thanks to Peggy Forbes for sharing her wisdom about the theater world and what it takes to run a regional theater.

I have great writer friends who are also terrific readers. Thanks to Lalita Tademy, Elizabeth Stark, Rosemary Graham, Nina Schuyler, Vicky Mlyniec, and Boris Fishman, who all read early drafts of this novel and helped me find my way.

I'm a very lucky writer to have landed with the agent Sally Wofford-Girand many years ago. She's smart and sharp and funny and wise and so very good at what she does. Thank you, Sally, again and again.

I owe a great deal to my brilliant editor, Jennifer Smith. She read an early draft of this novel and told me I had taken a wrong turn. I muttered many curse words under my breath while agreeing to try a new direction. And then, when I finally figured it out a few months later, I wrote her an email saying: *Damn you. You're right.* Thank you, Jen, for your keen vision— you could see the proper shape of my novel well before I could. And thank you for your gentle, lovely way of guiding me. I'm so glad you never heard all those bad words.

I try to attend a writers' residency every year—they feed my soul and offer me a remarkable chance to write without distraction. Brush Creek Arts in Wyoming deserves a lot of the credit for this novel. I wrote the first hundred pages in a two-week frenzy of creative energy while living there in my beautiful cabin. Then I returned almost a year later to rewrite the novel. Thank you to the Brush Creek Foundation for the Arts.

The folks at Ballantine and Random House make me very happy. I so appreciate the work of Libby McGuire, Kim Hovey, Jennifer Hershey, Hannah Elnan, Cindy Murray, Susan Corcoran, Maggie Oberrender, Janet Wygal, Dana Blanchette, and so many others who truly love to bring books into the world. Thanks for taking me in and treating me so well.

Many thanks to the Goddess of Web Design, Ilsa Brink.

Neal Rothman, thank you for all that you do for me, for us.

A Wedding in Provence

A Novel

ELLEN SUSSMAN

A Reader's Guide

A Conversation with Ellen Sussman
and Amanda Eyre Ward

Amanda Eyre Ward: Ellen, I love how *A Wedding in Provence* transported me to France. Can you talk about how the setting of Cassis inspired the story?

Ellen Sussman: I lived in Paris for five years when my daughters were babies. We'd vacation every summer in Provence. (I know—lucky me!) When I thought about writing a novel about a fiftysomething-year-old couple getting hitched, I knew immediately that the wedding would take place in Provence. I wanted a setting that was rich in sensory stimulation: The heat! The food! The smells! The light! That blue blue sea! Mix all that with love, and you've got a heady combination.

I had not visited Cassis until a few years ago. It's a charming town on the coast, less touristy than many of the towns along the Côte d'Azur. I fell for Cassis in a big way—in fact, I now dream of living there one day. When I walked in the mountains, when I kayaked in the calanques, when I feasted in one of the cafés along the sea, I could imagine my characters at my side, already coming to life in this fabulous setting.

AEW: I have started spending time choosing where each of my characters lives, even down to finding their house, where they buy their coffee, etc.

Did you visit Cassis for research, and if so, can you talk about how you research a setting? Do you walk around taking notes on the sky, or locate where each character will have a drink?

ES: On my first visit to Cassis, I just soaked it all up. I don't think I even took notes. But my senses were on high alert—I seemed suddenly able to see things, smell things, taste things with remarkable clarity. Then I wrote the first draft of the novel, pouring all of those observations and sensations into my story.

I went back to Cassis for a weeklong visit between draft one and two of *A Wedding in Provence*. (Yes, this kind of research is the most fun part of my job!) This time I knew what I was looking for. What did it sound like when it rained? What did it feel like to swim in that delicious sea? What might Carly have seen while sitting at the beach café in Cassis? (In fact, I did see a man surreptitiously taking photos of a lovely young topless woman on the beach—while his much older wife prepared a picnic for the two of them. And that went right into the novel!)

So some of what happens in that research week is planned and some is dumb luck. I hadn't thought of using the stormy weather in the novel until we experienced the wild winds of the mistral and I realized it was a perfect backdrop for the drama of my characters.

AEW: How does a novel come to you: fully formed, or in snippets? Does the character come first? Does this change for each novel?

ES: I never know very much about my novel when I'm first starting out. Sometimes it's a scene that gets me going—sometimes it's a character. But I never know what's going to happen at the end of the novel. I like working that way—it keeps me curious and interested. I'm on a quest; I need to find out what's going to happen. And I think that energy goes into the writing. I want my reader turning pages—and if I'm writing to discover, then they'll be reading to discover.

That makes for a wonderful first-draft experience. I give myself free rein to follow my characters anywhere. They dictate what happens—and I let them fumble their way through complicated situations. It's the second, third, and fourth drafts where the hard work takes place. Then I have to take a look at the world I've created and determine if I've shaped the novel well, if I've given the characters their full journeys, if I've explored this fictional world with depth and passion.

AEW: Any words of wisdom about plotting a book with love and relationships at its center?

ES: In *A Wedding in Provence,* I knew that I wanted to write a novel about a second chance at love. And I wanted to write about fifty-year-olds grappling with love and commitment and family. So I had one driving question that propelled me through the novel: How do you commit to love and marriage when you know so much about all the ways in which love fails?

I don't start writing a novel with answers—just questions. Again, I'm on a quest—I want to learn and discover rather than to report on what I already know.

Once I created Olivia and Brody as the central couple, with their questions about love, I thought, Let's shake up this world even more. So both of Olivia's daughters struggle with love. Brody's mother has just found out that her husband of fifty years has walked away from their marriage. Brody's best man is determined to never fall in love. Olivia's best friend discovers on the first night of this supposedly idyllic wedding weekend that her own husband has cheated on her. Can anyone get it right?

I gave myself a lot to work with. That's when the fun begins. I didn't know what would happen during this wedding weekend, but with so much conflict brewing, I was never at a loss to create drama on the page.

In the end, what did I learn about love? Maybe there is no real way to know that this time we'll get it right. In the end, we close our eyes and dive in. I'm a love junkie—I think we just go for it.

AEW: Do you write every day?

ES: Yes! I'm a very disciplined writer. I think it's crazy to wait for the muse to sit on my shoulder—I may be waiting a long time. Instead I show up and demand that she shows up too. So I work from nine till noon every day. And I write one thousand words a day. I treat it like a real job—I get dressed (changing from my yoga pajamas to my yoga clothes), plant my butt on my chair, don't answer the phone, disable the Internet. (There's a software program, Freedom, that enables me to do that. And I need it!) I'm a tough boss—if I haven't finished my word count by noon, then I march back into my office after lunch. But most days I've managed to hit one thousand words, and then I head to the hills for a hike with my dogs.

Some of the best writing gets done during my nonoffice hours. I'll take notes during that hike, or while waiting at the dentist's office, or in the middle of the night. Since I write daily, the fictional world swirls in my brain at all times. You might say my characters are my constant companions.

AEW: Now, you have two lovely daughters, and so does Olivia. Is the book at all autobiographical?

ES: No! Yes! No! Yes! Here are some of the similarities between *A Wedding in Provence* and my personal life. I got married for the second time—in France (though not in Cassis). I have two daughters, twenty-six and twenty-eight, the same ages as Nell and Carly. But that's about it—the rest is truly fiction. Nothing that happened in the novel happened at my wedding in France. (My girls were twelve and fourteen then. I'm quite sure there were none of the Nell/Carly sexual shenanigans at my wedding!)

My daughters are very different from each other—though not in the bad girl/good girl roles that Nell and Carly assume.

I've been fascinated by how siblings can be so strikingly different—as if they don't come from the same parents or the same set of familial experiences. I wanted to explore the sister bond, sibling rivalry, how kids define themselves in opposition to each other. In the end, I've created very different characters from my own daughters. But yes, my own very personal exploration fueled that quest.

And yes, the novel is peppered with tiny autobiographical moments. I really did turn the invisible key on my older daughter's forehead so that she could turn off her thoughts and go to sleep when she was a child. And yes, my husband and I once stayed at an inn in Provence where the owner's white retriever, Ulysse, became our lovable Rent-a-Dog for daily hikes.

AEW: What are you working on next?

ES: I'm a little superstitious about this—I don't talk about a new project until I've at least written a first draft. It's too fragile—or maybe I'm too fragile! If someone were to say: That's a lousy idea, I might trash the file and never look back. So I keep my characters in a tiny protective bubble—no one else knows them or what they're up to.

But I can say this: I'm trying to strike out in a new direction. The new novel takes place in San Francisco. And it's told in first person—I haven't done that before. I'm loving my characters—they're not like anyone I know. And so this journey—for them and for me—will take us places we've never been.

Thanks, Amanda, for taking the time to interview me. Great questions!

I'd love to recommend Amanda's books to all my readers. She's one of my favorite writers—if you don't already know her work, you're in for a great reading experience. Check out her latest: *The Same Sky.* You'll be wowed.

Questions and Topics for Discussion

1. *A Wedding in Provence* starts by introducing a happy couple on the way to their idyllic wedding. How did this affect your expectations for the book? Were you nervous about how events would unravel?

2. Nell is clearly a loose cannon. What were your initial thoughts when she decided to bring Gavin to the wedding? Did you think he was dangerous, or just a fun-loving, spontaneous stranger?

3. Were you surprised when Carly took off with Gavin? Why or why not?

4. In many ways Carly is Nell's opposite, but the two sisters end up attracted to the same man, however briefly. Is it possi-

ble that they aren't actually as different as they seem? Do you think they share any other similarities?

5. At the beginning of Chapter Sixteen, Olivia and Emily are discussing Nell's vulnerability. Was Emily's advice to Olivia helpful? How would you have suggested that Olivia manage her daughters' differences?

6. After learning that Sébastien cheated on Emily, Olivia is clearly rattled. She says "We're brave old fools. . . . We still choose love when we know everything that can happen," (page 19). Do you think a marriage can survive infidelity?

7. What did you think of Sam leaving Fanny after fifty-five years of marriage and refusing to come to Brody's wedding? Were you surprised when you found out why?

8. Throughout the novel, Olivia and Brody are faced with numerous obstacles that threaten to ruin their low-key wedding weekend. From Nell's surprise guest to Carly's disappearance and Sébastien's infidelity, which do you think caused the biggest stir? Why?

9. Of all the characters in the novel, which one did you most sympathize with?

10. Even though Olivia's big day is the backbone of the plot, the narrative rotates among her perspective and each of her daughters'. Was there ever a time when you felt drawn to one of the three points of view more than the others? When and why?

11. As Olivia and Brody get ready to commit to marriage, they witness their friends and family struggling with relationships. Is their love tested by these struggles? Do you think it's hard to say yes to love when we know everything that might go wrong in a marriage?

12. Of all the themes present in this novel—love, loss, starting fresh—which resonated with you the most? Why?

ELLEN SUSSMAN is the nationally bestselling author of the novels *On a Night Like This, French Lessons, The Paradise Guest House,* and *A Wedding in Provence.* She is the editor of two anthologies, *Bad Girls: 26 Writers Misbehave,* a *New York Times* Editors' Choice and a *San Francisco Chronicle* bestseller, and *Dirty Words: A Literary Encyclopedia of Sex.* She has published numerous essays and short stories. Ellen teaches creative writing both in private classes and through Stanford Continuing Studies. She has two daughters and lives with her husband in Northern California.

www.EllenSussman.com
Facebook.com/ellensussman
@ellensussman

ABOUT THE TYPE

This book was set in Fournier, a typeface named
for Pierre-Simon Fournier (1712–68), the young-
est son of a French printing family. He started
out engraving woodblocks and large capitals,
then moved on to fonts of type. In 1736 he began
his own foundry and made several important
contributions in the field of type design; he is
said to have cut 147 alphabets of his own crea-
tion. Fournier is probably best remembered as
the designer of St. Augustine Ordinaire, a face
that served as the model for the Monotype Cor-
poration's Fournier, which was released in 1925.

Chat.
Comment.
Connect.

Visit our online book club community at
Facebook.com/RHReadersCircle

Chat

Meet fellow book lovers and discuss what you're reading.

Comment

Post reviews of books, ask—and answer—thought-provoking
questions, or give and receive book club ideas.

Connect

Find an author on tour, visit our author blog, or invite one of
our 150 available authors to chat with your group on the phone.

Explore

Also visit our site for discussion questions, excerpts, author
interviews, videos, free books, news on the latest releases,
and more.

Books are better with buddies.
Facebook.com/RHReadersCircle

RANDOM HOUSE